SEA CELL

SEA CELL

Chuck Hile

Waterside Productions

Printed in the United States of America

First Printing, 2021

ISBN-13: 978-1-954968-10-3 print edition
ISBN-13: 978-1-954968-11-0 ebook edition

Waterside Productions
2055 Oxford Ave
Cardiff, CA 92007
www.waterside.com

TABLE OF CONTENTS

CHAPTER 1

The barista was frantically putting together any number of morning drinks that all had a coffee influence. He looked up from the counter and focused his attention on a business on the other side of the mall. She was due any minute now. As if on autopilot, right on time, the cherry red Ferrari slipped into a parking space in front of the Ultimate Spa center just across the parking lot from Starbucks. It was eight o'clock Monday morning. It was the same routine every day Monday through Thursday. It was the highlight of Chris Cummings's mornings on those days. Another rash of orders were placed that he needed to attend to, so the arousing few seconds he just experienced would be revisited on his break. Occasionally, the Ferrari driver would walk across the parking area and order one of the more exotic concoctions "to go." He made it a point to not wait on her, even if he had to fake an emergency trip to the bathroom. A low profile was his intent. He had conjured up so many imaginary situations involving her that he was almost ready to implode. He was obsessed with that thought. *I'll think of something*, he thought. *I have to or I'll go crazy.* He was preoccupied with the constant thought of what he could do. It was an obsession that he actually enjoyed in a twisted psychological way.

While Chris was staring at a row of cups in front of him and reading the inscriptions of what the customers had ordered, he stole a glance in the direction of the spa.

Chrystal Townsend had just opened the door of the Ferrari. As she stepped out, her shapely legs could be seen as she exited a car that must have cost a fortune. She was wearing very short shorts. Most of the regular male population inside the spa enjoyed her sexuality and grace as she made her way into the spa. They all had their X-rated thoughts. Many of the women had an air of indifference as they pretended not to be aware of this personification of femininity as she strode into the spa, wishing to themselves, "I'd kill if I could look anything like that."

Meanwhile the "work-out-oholics" pressed on with their routines. The hum and grinding of workout equipment permeated the atmosphere in this Malibu, California workout facility. Each moved to their selection of self-inflicted pain to meet their physical fitness goals. Chris, across the parking lot, who did not live in the area, was busy trying to stay ahead of the curve as he quickly and efficiently prepared the tsunami of orders that never seemed to end. He does manage to sneak a glance or two toward the Ferrari from time to time.

It was Monday morning and summertime in Southern California.

CHAPTER 2

Chris removed his Starbucks apron from around his neck, which had his name embroidered in white across the left side. It was noon and his shift was over. His car was parked some distance from the store. It was policy that staff did not occupy parking spaces close to the store. As he made his way to his car, he looked to see if the Ferrari was still at the spa. It never was, but he looks anyway. He pulled out of the lot and made his way to the Pacific Coast Highway (PCH to locals). As he entered the southbound ramp, he gauged the traffic that would dictate the time it would take to get to Santa Monica. The highway, as the name implies, is a north/south road with the ocean on the west side and mountains and hills to the east. It's truly a magnificent and beautiful drive, but has distractions, traffic, and occasional mudslides. During this twenty-mile drive, Chris's thought processes were often about the Ferrari Girl. The longer the drive, the more time he had to embrace his obsession. He knew he had to do something about it, and he would. During the drive on this particular day, he was lip-synching away, oblivious to the occasional stares from passing drivers or a beep of a horn as he drove well below the speed limit—a freeway no-no in Los Angeles County. His main thought today was to carefully take his time planning ways to address what do about the beauty with the red car. "I will not rush. I will not make a mistake." He reduced his speed. His destination was now in sight. He pulled into the Santa Monica City College parking lot.

While his parents were alive, he honored their wishes to enroll in school. He had no preenrollment idea of what he wanted to do academically. Nor did he have any idea what he wanted to if he did graduate. Today his mind was not on what his parents would have wanted him to achieve in school, but instead on the sexy lady across the parking lot. Since he had to take afternoon classes, finding a parking spot was not an issue. More often than not, he parked in the same spot. A smile crossed his face as he eased his car between the faded white lines that designated the confines of where he could park. He duly noted the buildup of oil drippings that were well embedded in the asphalt as he eased into the space. *Most of that oil is mine*, he thought. The almost daily reminder of his engine leaking oil was the impetus of him taking an adult evening class. Initially, the course was to learn about engines for economical purposes, but he started to develop another use for the knowledge as it fed into his obsession. He had an hour and a half to kill before his first class, so he partially opened all his windows to allow the ocean breeze to gently enter the car. He set the alarm on his watch to go off in one hour. He leaned back in the car seat, closed his eyes, and drifted off to sleep, visualizing the essence of the Ferrari Girl.

Beep, beep, the wrist watch alarm activated. He had been in a deep sleep and dreaming about his parents whom he loved and cherished. *Well, here I am, mom and dad, heading off to class, just as you wished.* It really was annoying to be awakened because he was very tired after a hard and busy shift at Starbucks. He wanted the dream of his parents to continue. Now awake, he partially raised each window, but not all the way. He left just enough space for the breeze to enter his car, but not enough room for someone to reach in and unlock the car. Frequently, students had been robbed or had their cars broken into. The interior items of choice were stereos and speakers. Satisfied that his Camry was secured, he carefully opened the car door and was careful not to step in any oil spots. He hitched up his backpack and started across the parking lot to his first class. Kinesiology. It was his favorite subject.

The academic day would down and twenty-two-year-old Chris made his way to his parking spot. He looked westward toward the sun, and just like his wristwatch alarm, it was right on schedule as it started to slip toward the horizon. Something else right on schedule was the just before five o'clock evening traffic. It would be slow going on the drive north.

The outskirts of Port Hueneme became more distinctive as Chris scanned the horizon. He'd be home soon. Today, the drive was not the nightmare he expected. The drive, just under forty miles, was not difficult. Even though he had been up since four o'clock this morning, he felt alert and still had plenty of energy as he turned into the cul-de-sac. It was an area that was once agricultural and was now in its infancy of becoming residential. There were only three other homes on the street, and they were a considerable distance from each other. It was very quiet. There was just one dim streetlight providing just enough illumination to alert people who had accidentally turned onto the street that it was the end of the line and they needed to turn around. He pulled into his driveway and parked under a large mulberry tree that cast a canopy of tree limbs and foliage over much of the house and driveway. It was a messy tree. During the fruit bearing season, the ground under and around the tree is marked with purple stains caused by the rotting berries. When he parked, he delayed getting out of the car. In a moment of reflection, he recalled how his mom used to make delicious mulberry jam with the berries. Now home, he got out of the car, walked to the back door, and entered the empty, quiet, depressing house. It had the perpetual aura of emptiness.

CHAPTER 3

It had been three years since he lost his parents. It seemed like a lifetime ago. There was not a day that passed without him reflecting on what was. He was still in high school when his father told him that they would leaving Oxnard and moving to Port Mugu. He learned that his parents decided to buy an old house that was on land that they could develop. They would tear down the existing home, build three homes, then sell two and live in the other one. Fate stepped in to dash those dreams and ideas. The house of depression never got razed, but was truly a candidate for the wrecking ball. He had decided that the home would not be torn down. Another use for the house was starting to develop in his mind.

Sitting in an overstuffed chair that had multiple stains embedded in the fabric as well crumbs from any number of items he had ingested over the past three years, he looked westward at the horizon. He never tired looking at the ocean. The downside was that it brought back so many good memories of sailing and fishing with his father that would never happen again. His mind wandered as he visualized some of the things he had been taught. Chris was especially proud of how capable he was at navigation and engine repair, as well as his ability to utilize the wind when under sail. Apparent wind flow from true wind. The skill of tacking efficiently. His dad was a great teacher. Of all the things he loved about the sea, he put peacefulness, solitude, serenity, and peace of mind at the top of the list. He realized that he must have drifted off and phased into a light sleep when he was awoken by a car making a U-turn in the cul-de-sac and the car's headlights lit up the room and its soiled upholstery.

There's no such thing as planned meals or household schedules for the house under the mulberry tree. Chris flicked on the small and old TV set as he passed by on the way to the kitchen. There was some leftover takeout food in the fridge that he decided to eat cold. He grabbed a plastic bottle of Smartwater and headed back to his stuffed chair. He spent a lot of time in that chair. It was where he reflected a great deal on what had happened and what might happen. The thought du jour tonight was what had happened to his parents. He eased into the chair. He nibbled on some tasteless food and took an occasional sip of water as he stared out at the Pacific Ocean and the twinkling of lights that rimmed the coastline. In this reflective mood, he let his mind wander back to the day he got the news that his parents were missing at sea.

CHAPTER 4

Chris wiggled and squirmed his body into the well-worn crevices of the chair's upholstery as he continued thinking back to the time his life flipped upside down. Reflectively he recalled "the phone call." His mind wandered back to the events, conversations, and activities that took place after the call occurred.

The radio call from the Port Hueneme Coast Guard station had activated and was promptly answered. The caller was the captain of a commercial fishing boat and advised them that he had noticed a sailboat that seemed to be drifting in an unusual pattern without indication that it was under anyone's control. It had an American flag in place, aft of the common area. He added that the anchor had not been dropped and there did not seem to be anyone aboard. He advised the coast guard of his position, which was about forty miles southwest of Ensenada, Mexico. He agreed to standby until they could dispatch a helicopter or vessel to check it out.

What appeared to be an abandoned Gulf 32 sailboat had been boarded by coast guard sailors who confirmed that there was no one on the vessel. All the authentic identification relative to ownership had been located. Once that was established, it was to be towed to San Diego for further processing and evaluation.

While the sailboat was en route to San Diego, Chris was contacted and advised that the boat would be studied for clues as why there was no one aboard. The nineteen-year-old was so upset and shaken by the devastating news, he could hardly breathe or speak. Barely audible and pale because of the shock, he somehow managed to tell the voice on the phone that he would fly to San Diego and help out in any way he possibly could. He was flummoxed and barely coherent as the bad news consumed his physical and mental being. With the movements of a zombie and in a trance-like state, he departed for the airport to face the reality that he was now parentless, and what appeared to be a ghost sailboat. He really had no one to turn to for comfort, advice, or help. Neither of his parents had brothers or sisters, and both sets of grandparents were deceased. Now, on his way south, he was the personification of "alone."

Commander Nelson had entered the coast guard office and approached Chris. "I am the officer in charge of the events and circumstances regarding your family's sailboat, and I would like to ask you some questions."

"Okay," said Chris.

"Was the marriage of your mom and dad okay? Any marital problems that you are aware of?"

"It was a great marriage. I never saw them fight or get mad at each other. They were solid people that got along well with each other."

"Was the boat insured? What is the current value of the boat? Did they have any life insurance? If so, who is the beneficiary?"

"I'm not sure about any life insurance. I know the boat was insured." Gulf 32 sailboats were worth $40,000 to $50,000.

"Were your parents in good health?"

"Yes, as far as I know. They seldom went to a doctor."

"We have studied the boat from stem to stern and could not find anything out of order. Truthfully, we have no idea what occurred. Could you speculate on that topic?"

"That's all I have been thinking about since I heard from the coast guard. My dad was a great sailor. A good teacher who always insisted on being safe at sea. Maybe they were both at the rail and one of them leaned over too far and started to fall and the other tried to stop the fall and they both tumbled overboard. For the past few days, the weather was spotty and perhaps a rough wave hit the boat and they were caught by surprise and washed over the side. I don't think I'll ever know what happened. I just can't believe it even happened. Did you do a search of the area?"

"We did a ten-mile radius search from where the boat was found. We searched by helicopter and seacraft. During the search, we did note a lot of shark activity. Other than that, we did not find anything untoward."

"What do we do now, commander?"

"We will continue our evaluation and coordination with local law enforcement. It's beginning to look like an accidental mishap, and at this time we do not see any criminal aspects surrounding the disappearance of your parents. If you can stay in the area for a few days, we should be able to release the boat to you. Are you qualified to sail the boat back to its home port?"

"Yes. I have sailed the boat alone on numerous occasions over the last few years. I can handle the sails alone. I can fix engines and have navigation skills. I know everything about the boat and would have no problem sailing her back to Port Hueneme."

"Okay Chris, we will keep in touch. Leave a contact number with the clerk. Thanks for the visit and I wish you the best."

Five days later, the phone had rung at the Horton Hotel, and the coast guard call was passed along to Chris's room. It was the officer in charge of the investigation of the mysterious situation regarding his parents. He advised Chris that they had concluded their evaluation of the situation and foul play was ruled out. The boat would be released to him. He ended the conversation by telling him the final entry into their report would be that the Cummings Cruiser was found adrift at sea, unoccupied, no findings as to why. Case closed. What the officer had not told Chris was that they suspected a double suicide had taken place.

The wakeup call from the hotel desk rang and Chris answered instantly. It was five o'clock in the morning. He wanted to get the sailboat released as early as possible because it would be a long sail home. It was a short drive to the coast guard headquarters from the hotel. He beat the early morning commuters, so the scenic drive was short. He wished that had been the case for the never-ending red tape he had to wade through before he could push off from the dock and raise the mainsail, snag some wind, and start the ocean voyage home.

As he continued his recollection of those awful days, he was disturbed when a car made a U-turn on his street and the headlights flashed across his face, causing him to stir and interrupt his memory of that time. He didn't want to wake up. He closed his eyes and continued thinking about the sail home. "Now, where was I in my memory process?" he said to himself. "Oh yes, the sail home."

After he left the harbor, he had tacked the boat so that he could catch the south wind on the northbound sail. It was a brisk wind and it should allow him a straight sail home. Little, if no tacking, was what he had anticipated, so he locked in the automatic control of the helm so he did not have to man the helm during the entire sail. Moving along at six knots, he estimated the trip would take about twenty-five hours. He knew it would be a long and lonely time. As the seconds ticked on, memories of those times past flashed through his mind just like a heartbeat. They just came coming. One after another. Dad at the helm. Wind blowing against his face and his hair flowing as he faced the oncoming wind. Mom in the galley creating culinary delights. Dad yelling out instructions. "Faster on the tack, watch out for the boom." The recall state was so real he thought it was really happening.

When a second car made a U-turn and the headlights once again illuminated the room, he discontinued his recollection of the past. He looked out the window at the streetlight and made a mental note to contact the city to see if a new sign could be installed at the entrance to the cul-de-sac that read "No Outlet."

CHAPTER 5

It was another Monday. A work day. It was still dark as Chris started going through his usual routine at the start of each work day. The house was dark and sterile—lifeless, really. He was young and had no interest in keeping a neat or orderly home. It was very cluttered, and the sanitation was borderline. He often reflected on how it used to look. *Those days are long gone*, he thought to himself. He was lonely. He wanted friends and someone he could share his feelings with, but he seemed unable to allow that to happen. He protected his psyche by accepting the label *loner*. He had made some feeble efforts to cultivate friends at work, but it never seemed to work out. He was an introvert and had no problem with that label. He was not comfortable in the company of loud and verbal people. It was a vexation. He had often thought to himself that was why he loved the serene peacefulness of the ocean. He'd rather hear the sound of water slapping against the prow of the sailboat than listen to the prattle of others about topics that held no interest to him. Chris glanced at his watch and realized it was time to get on the PCH and head down the coast to Malibu. His hormones switched into high gear as the imagery of the Ferrari Girl kicked in during the drive. He loved the excitement and how aroused he became thinking about her. She was his invisible traveling companion and it made for a sweet, arousing drive.

During the drive down the coast, Chris had a heart-to-heart talk with himself. The topic: his obsession with the woman—the knockout sex goddess—he thought about constantly, and what to do about it. He had to decide if he was willing to do almost anything to satisfy his lust and desire to have her. When she parked her ultra-expensive car and swung open her door to exit the car, he only saw her for about ten seconds before she entered the spa. It was a tease. It was driving him crazy. Before pulling into the Starbucks parking lot, he took a deep breath and slowly exhaled. The decision. *She will be mine.* He entered the coffee shop and felt as if he had just been empowered with a meaningful purpose, and now it was time to get on with it. Now goal-oriented, he was eager to start planning the action he would take. He was euphoric and excited.

Now that Chris had accepted that he *would* have the Ferrari Girl, he needed to get dead serious on how he was going to make it happen. The first thing at the top of his list was time. What he needed to establish was a realistic time frame. It was now the start of summer. He didn't know if she was returning or going back to college. Would the end of summer affect her local habits and location? Would she leave the area? There were a lot of unknowns, that's for sure. Some of the following details that required immediate study and thought were running through his mind. He started a list.

1. Time: Five months
2. How to affect the abduction
3. Money
4. Post-abduction survival
5. Avoid being a suspect
6. *Blank entry*

It was Tuesday. He left a message with a realtor to call him. He decided that the sale of the property and the amount of money he would get was vital to ensure the success of his fantasy. Just taking the first step in his plan is exhilarating.

Wednesday. Chris gave a two-week notice that he would end his Starbucks employment. Reason for leaving: extensive travel. After his shift ended, he started researching where he could enroll in a photography class. Each step in his planning made him feel vital and full of life. Deep down he knows it's crazy, but he felt there was nothing he could do about it. The force that was pushing him was so powerful that it was taking over his psyche. It was an avalanche of evil, disturbing, and twisted thoughts that were controlling his very being. He had now started the implementation of what he hoped would end his worry about controlling the most beautiful creation he had ever seen. His euphoria was limitless. Social unacceptability would not factor into his planning. It was time to act.

CHAPTER 6

The early morning coastal fog covered the coastline and was slowly giving way to the first rays of the sun that were now easing over the Malibu Mountains and nudging the fog seaward. It was a peaceful and pleasant adjustment, watching the grey mist evaporate ever-so-slowly and silently, allowing the sunshine to say good morning to the affluent denizens of the city of Malibu.

Located about three-quarters of a mile away from the ocean's edge was the estate of the Townsend family. The entire property was located on a hillside with sweeping views of the city and the Pacific Ocean. Privacy was assured by a private winding road that snaked its way up the partially wooded asphalt road off of a community road at the base of the estate. The 7,500-square-foot home sat on five acres of land and was located on the western edge of the site. The value of the home and property would certainly exceed $15 to $21 million, if not more. All the amenities of a home with that value were in place. The fog wasn't the only thing that was affected by the sun making its daily appearance.

There was a small ruffling of the silk sheets that was slowly increasing in movement. The outline of a woman's body could be seen by the indentation and molding of a sheet as it draped over the curvature of Chrystal Townsend as she began to wake up. She slowly stretched and twisted her body and gave in to the inevitable—it was time to wake up and get up. For a few seconds, she looked up at the fifteen-foot ceiling and then rolled over on her right side so she could see the ocean. The view was unobstructed as she stared at the blue mass. She delayed getting out of the bed because the reality was that there really was no urgency to taking on the day. She continued to stare at her next-door neighbor, the Pacific Ocean. The moment was interrupted by a large formation of pelicans gracefully gliding south. Not a single one was moving its wings. The north wind was what provided the power source for one of nature's most beautiful airborne creatures. The uniformity and gracefulness of the formation was hypnotic to watch and enjoy. The pelicans slid across the horizon and glided out of sight. Chrystal's feet touched the floor and she stood. She stretched her body and gracefully walked to another part of the one-thousand-square-foot bedroom. *What a fantastic way to start my day*, she thought.

As she neared the three-foot by ten-foot fish aquarium, she stopped. Something she often did. The aquarium was installed on the top of cabinetry that extended across a large portion of the room and served as a room divider. It contained numerous tropical fish. Each species was thoughtfully chosen for their compatibility with each other. The water was pristine. Chrystal enjoyed watching the brilliant kaleidoscope of the colors of the fish as they went about their daily routines—especially at feeding time. The placid water exploded with the swarming of the larger fish as they swooped to the floating food bits as they drifted downward, inhaling the larger pieces. Some of the fish that were smaller than an eyelash and almost transparent seemed comfortable swimming about nibbling at what seemed like nothing, but there must have been something. When in a contemplative mood, Chrystal often reflected on something that she and the brilliant hues of the fish share in common. She stared at them because they are beautiful and pleasing to observe. With no intention of being egotistical, she feels that more often than not, she is viewed in a manner just like when she looks at the fish. By anyone's standards, she is beautiful. Beauty can be a blessing, but at times made her feel uncomfortable. She left the fish tank and sashayed to the vanity for some last minute touch ups before she reviewed her schedule for the day.

Descending the stairs, Chrystal could see her mother in the kitchen area sitting at a table drinking coffee and working the crossword puzzle. She was doing the devils tattoo with her left hand and appeared to be in deep thought.

"Hi, Mom. Are you stuck? What word are you looking for and how many letters?"

"Okay, smarty. Give me a word for beauty. Eight letters."

Chrystal feigned confusion. "Chrystal," she replied.

They both laughed. It was a little game they played. After the initial levity ebbed, they shared their agendas for the day. Her mother was very involved with several charities. She not only made sizable donations to some of them, but was on several advisory boards. Both had their daily agendas, and her mom would follow through on her social schedule and Chrystal would be off doing her usual Tuesday schedule. During the summer, Chrystal had a predicable list of activities. The spa, nails, Pilates.

"Can't be late," said her mom.

"You know me, Mom. Miss Punctuality. Gotta run." She took a sip of her mom's coffee, gave her a kiss on her cheek, and headed out the door to the Ferrari.

CHAPTER 7

As the cherry red and super powerful Ferrari raced down the winding road away from the Townsend estate, Chrystal was enjoying the thrill of pushing the speed machine to its limits as she negotiated the sharp turns of their private road. It was exhilarating. She loved speed and the excitement of driving fast. Now following the speed limit on the public road, she headed for the PCH. As she neared the mall entrance, she revved the engine and geared down as she approached the spa.

Approximately one hundred yards away was a Camry parked near a dumpster that was located in a spot where very few cars drive by or park. Inside of the car and across the wind shield was a sun screen that had been placed on the dashboard. It blocked anyone from looking into the car. The windows had been slightly tinted. Chris had placed his camera on the dashboard and the lens was aimed at the spa. Chris had cut out a small circle in the sun screen so the rather long and powerful lens could be aimed at anything he wished to photograph. It would be hardly noticeable to a person who might casually glance in his direction. He arrived about twenty minutes before his sex obsession was scheduled to arrive. He smiled. *She is so predictable*, he thought. He had been in this spot for the last three Tuesday mornings. It was a few minutes before eight o'clock. Softly, he said to the car interior, "she'll be here any minute now." He lightly rubbed his hands together and then double-checked his camera to ensure that it was focused and aimed at the target area. He knew he only had about fifteen seconds to click off shots—the approximate time it took for her to get out the car and make the short walk to the entrance. Those fifteen seconds were exhilarating. His pulse was picking up speed and his breath was starting to become more rapid. He knew she would be here any moment.

He heard the Ferrari before he saw it. His finger was poised to quickly photograph her getting out of the car. Hopefully, the door would open and she would extend her body reaching for something in the car. That would allow him a little more time to get some shots of her fantastic legs that were simply perfection. Today he was lucky. After she opened the door, she contorted her body in such a fashion that caused her to extend her physique as she reached for something in what would be the back seat area in a conventional car. This caused the entire length of her body to extend, revealing the graceful and sexy shapes of this beautiful woman. One whom he plans on having and controlling. She is out of the car now. He couldn't click the shutter fast enough. He took a couple more shots as she entered the spa. The photo op for this morning was over. The best part would happen soon—developing the film. He took down the sun screen, neatly folded it, and tossed it in the back seat. As he pulled out of the parking, lot he doubled-checked to confirm that there were no security cameras. He had checked for that before, but it just reassured him that it was still the case. His mantra was to keep a low profile and prevent authorities from connecting the dots that could lead a trail to him in the future. Of paramount importance was that he would never be filmed in an area where Townsend lived or visited.

Motoring northbound on the PCH, Chris was oblivious to the traffic flow as he poked along in the right-hand lane. He hadn't noticed a single frown or negative expression of the drivers passing on his left as they stared or glared at him when passing. His brain was racing overtime. He was so preoccupied with everything he must do and do flawlessly that it was consuming him. He was so deep in thought that he missed his off ramp to the Port Hueneme Marina where his boat was moored. Two more miles up the highway, he made a driving correction and got himself on track to get off at the correct ramp. Now at the marina parking lot, he eased his car into an empty parking space. He turned off the ignition and reflected on what he had done and what remained to be done on this exciting yet scary adventure he had embarked on.

During the past three weeks, he had been quite active. He reached into the glove compartment and grabbed a pencil and a piece of paper. He started a list of his activities to ensure that he was on track to assure success in his daring plan.

1. He sold his home during the last few days of June. He sold it for around 25 percent lower than its value. It was a ten-day escrow and all cash. If there were comments about the speed of the sale or inquires and questions, he'd simply tell them that he planned to sail around the world.
2. He stocked his boat with extra amounts of everything needed for a long trip at sea. Gas, food, water, and so forth.
3. He checked the requirements to fly a drone for recreational use. He checked that off as done.
4. He had lined up the sale of his car. Sell cheap. Cash only.
5. He bought a bicycle.
6. He had extra sails made for the trip. They would be ready before he sailed.
7. He had moved onto the boat full time and had let it be known to the other marina denizens that he would set sail next Tuesday.
8. He rented a storage space near the marina and paid one year's rent in advance.

He stared at the to-do list and felt he had or will have completed everything by the time he and Chrystal were together. He slowly put the list on the passenger's seat and gazed out at the marina. A melancholy mood set in as he reflected on the years he and his parents had been a part of this community, which was about to end soon. It had been such a huge part of his life. Looking out at the wharf, he looked toward his boat at the end of the dock and saw a long line of masts with their sails down gently rocking and bobbing from side to side as small ripples of water nudged against their hulls. Some had small colorful banners flapping in the soft and warm breeze. He could hear the metal guide lines that served various purposes hitting against each other and producing sounds very familiar to sailors. He could see some boat owners performing minor repairs and maintenance. Some were using flatbed carts to move supplies from the entrance up or down the dock. A few seagulls were perched on boats where the owners were absent. They are the keenest of observers. A microscopic piece of something edible puts them into instant action. To the chagrin of the boating world, they are a part of their family. As he looked beyond the protective harbor, he could see a few boats heading out to the open sea. He noted that the wind was coming out of the north. No whitecaps, but enough wind that the boats would not have to use their motors and could unfurl the sails. It was a beautiful sight to watch the sails expand and catch the wind. His melancholy mood began to fade and he returned to the here and now. He was anxious to start developing the film in the makeshift darkroom he had developed on the boat. He put the strap of the camera over his shoulder and enthusiastically walked to his boat with high expectations of the pictures he took of his obsession.

As was his habit, he clicked on his small television set and started the film development process. The cacophony from the TV helped offset his loneliness. He could hear it in the background, but really didn't care what was being said. While he was in the process of developing the shots of Chrystal he took this morning, he stopped at once when he heard an announcement on the local television station.

"Congratulations are in order for Chrystal Townsend, a recent graduate of Stanford University, for being accepted to the prestigious University of Oxford in England to continue her studies in the field of causes and treatment for multiple sclerosis, or MS." Chris did not finish the development of the film. Instead, he turned on his computer to get more details about the troubling news he just heard on the television. He Googled the story and was shocked to learn that she would be leaving for England in the near future. The term "near future" was like a hand grenade had just exploded. He was stunned. He must expedite all phases of the abduction of the Ferrari Girl.

CHAPTER 8

It was Sunday morning in Southern California, and the rays of sunshine were erasing the shadows that lingered from the wee hours of the night just before sunrise. The Townsend household was starting to stir. Another gorgeous California morning was making its debut. The awaking ritual commences. The silk sheets were starting to wiggle and crinkle as Chrystal slowly stretched beneath them. She turned on her side to view the morning and the majestic view of the Pacific. It's a sight she had enjoyed her entire life. There were no Pelican formations this morning. Instead, she fixated on the family of three doves that had stopped in for a visit and were waddling and cooing, their heads bobbing up and down as they walked across her small bedroom balcony, from time to time pecking at invisible specks that the human eye could not see on the marble floor. The melodic doves' conversations and sounds were pleasant to hear. They were friendly and appeared secure. It was a great way to start her day. She turned her body so she was now looking up at the vaulted ceiling. As she stared at the ceiling, she made a mental note of things she had to do before she left for England on Wednesday. At the top of the list is the guests coming to the house for her bon voyage party. She was especially delighted that her aunt who had an advanced stage of MS would be there that night. She made a mental note to spend time with her. She had multiple sclerosis and could hardly speak. Chrystal knew that her aunt would have written a few appropriate comments that would be nearly impossible to read, but she will make a big fuss over the notes. She heard her mom moving around in the kitchen, and looked away from the ceiling. She smiled and made a note to remember to tell her mom she would not be around in the mornings to help her with her crossword puzzle. She flipped back the covers and stepped out of bed.

When she walked by the fish tank, she took a quick glance at her aquatic friends. Now was the time to enjoy them on one of her few remaining days before she left.

While Chrystal was starting her routines as the day unfolded, less than a mile away, a drone was photographing the surrounding area of the Townsend property. Great care was being taken to ensure that it would not be noticed by anyone in or around the house. Chris would study it diligently after he had filmed the general area. He had only physically been in the area one time, and he rode his bike on that occasion. The "fly around"—not "over"—ended and Chris was now one step closer to acquiring his most prized possession. The mere thought of her being "his" activated his testosterone juices. The excitement and thrill of what was about to happen was fantastic. As he reigned in the drone, he thought to himself, *Hurry up, Tuesday.* Before he left the area, he looked around and felt that he had not been noticed by anyone. He had made it a point to not be in the area very long. He was there for less than ten minutes.

After returning to the Cummings Cruiser, Chris reviewed the drone photos and was satisfied with the aerial recon. It would be helpful. He reflected on all the planning and things he had done to date. The next step would have to wait until Tuesday. He filed the photos the drone provided and hopped up the seven steps to topside and lounged on the cushions that were in place in the aft of the boat. It's a Chamber of Commerce day. He tried to relax. As he was doing so, he closed his eyes and drifted into a reflective mood. He slipped into that feeling you have just before you drift off to a deep sleep. He was still semi awake, but he knew that sleep was closing in. Before he succumbed to drifting off to a dreamy world, he contemplated scenario after scenario about the activities and acts that would occur once he had his obsession aboard. He doesn't want those images and thoughts to end, but there is an interruption. It causes him to lose that drowsy feeling and pay attention to the unexpected intruder. The intruder is his conscience. *Am I really going to follow through with all this?*

Chris opened his eyes, rolled over on his back, and looked straight up at the thirty-foot main mast, sans sail, stretching skyward and seeming to be perched on a soft, fluffy, white pristine cloud drifting by. He continued to stare at the mast as it gently swayed back and forth. Its rhythmic movement was hypnotic, and he succumbed to a most pleasant sleep with a trace of a smile on his face as he subconsciously imagined the exciting events that would soon take place.

CHAPTER 9

Tuesday. Chrystal started her early-morning routines as she prepped for the spa for the last time for quite a while. Tomorrow she would be airborne. Destination: England. She tossed some miscellaneous items in her workout bag and descended the stairs. It's off to the spa. She stopped by the kitchen to give her mother a peck on the cheek and a cheery ta-ta. She announced that she had a few goodbyes to take care of as well as some errands to run, so she would not be home until midafternoon. She opened the patio sliding door and headed for the garage. Mrs. Townsend heard the Ferrari engine roar to life. She watched the taillights fade away as her daughter left the property. She thought to herself that she would really miss her daughter and wished she wasn't going to be so far away for such a long time. She diverted her attention away from the window and continued working the crossword puzzle.

Long before Chrystal woke up, Chris had been busy getting ready for what he "had to do." After all the hours and weeks of organizing and planning, it was now going to happen. He did a quick mental review and was satisfied that he was ready for the abduction. He left the wharf and went to the nearby parking lot reserved for the boat owners. He had put his bicycle on top of the Camry the previous evening. He checked to ensure that it was secured, got behind the wheel, and started the drive to Malibu. Summer was just starting, and daylight started erasing the night around five-thirty in the morning. He was tense. He had told himself over and over every second he was driving to be sure to not violate any driving laws. It seemed like he had only been on the road a few minutes and the twenty-mile drive was over. He was now in the Townsend home vicinity. It was nearly six o'clock.

Less than a mile away was a makeshift parking area where the locals parked when they went for hikes through some narrow canyons and mountains that bordered the Malibu area. It wasn't paved. The hikers parked their cars just about any place that appealed to them. Rarely were the cars very close to one another. When Chris arrived there was only one car in sight. He selected a spot near a pine tree just a few yards away from the paved road that served as an entrance to the area. It was not possible to park in such a way that his car was out of sight, but it was partially covered by a few of the low-lying branches from a tree. Satisfied with the location, he ventured away from the car and walked on the asphalt road toward a stand of trees and snapped off a small branch from a eucalyptus tree. Back at his car, he tossed the branch near the driver's side of the car. He then removed his bike from the car and walked around the car so that he was partially out of sight from the entrance road. He had acquired all the accoutrements that the more serious cyclists wear. After cinching up his helmet, he removed a satchel from the back seat, which had a plastic lining that would prevent liquids from leaking or spilling. It had a leather strap that he put over his shoulder. He looked at his watch and realized that the time for his preparation period was taking longer that he planned. It was time to cycle to the Townsend road which was a about a mile away. He pulled up the bandana that covered his face and peddled away from the area. No one had seen him enter the area or leave. Perfect.

7:30 a.m. Chris turned off the frontage road and cycled close to three hundred yards on the Townsend road. He partially disassembled his cycle. He detached both wheels and then arranged them to look as though they were still a part of the frame. He then laid down on the road and staged the scene as if he had fallen and was hurt. She should be speeding down the road any minute. He heard her coming. When Chrystal eased around the last turn in the road, she immediately starting slowing down. She was being waved down by an obviously injured bicyclist who needed help. He was waving to her to stop. She did. She exited her car and hurried to the accident site.

"Oh my gosh, are you alright?" She asked.

Chris's replied, faking serious pain. "No, I think I might have broken my ankle. Will you be kind enough to help me get off to the side of the road?"

"Of course. How do you want me to help?"

"If you could just help me stand up that would be nice." He continued his pseudo pain antics.

As Chrystal bent over to help him to his feet, she did not notice that he slowly had removed his bandana and slipped it into a satchel that he had filled with chloroform. Chris had done extensive research regarding the anesthetic properties of chloroform and learned that it does not take immediate effect as so often portrayed in movies or on television. It can take three to five minutes. He also learned that it evaporates fairly quickly, so the faster it is applied the better.

Chrystal bent over and asked, "Do you want me to lift you up by putting my arms under your shoulders?"

"Please. I'll try to stand up as you do." The fake pain was intensifying.

The instant she reached for him, he violently pulled her hair and twisted her head so he could hold her in a modified choke hold. He placed the chloroform-soaked bandana over her face. Her body reacted instinctively and violently. She flayed, twisted, and turned. She tried mightily to pull his arm away from the chokehold, but he was too strong. She tried to scream but the only sound that emitted was muffled. She felt her strength failing because whatever was on the rag was starting to take effect. The resistance was more than Chris had expected. She was in good shape and fought hard. He had to end the physical aspect of controlling her, so he squeezed violently in the thorax area to try to subdue her even if he had to choke her out before the chloroform took full effect. The clock was ticking away. About two minutes into the act, her resistance started to ebb. Her body started to go limp. In a few more seconds she in fact did stop fighting and fell into an unconsciousness. Satisfied that he could release his physical control of Chrystal, he laid her next to the passenger door. He had planned on putting his bike behind the seats but there was not enough room. He made a quick decision to lay the seat back down as far as he could—which was not very far—put Chrystal in a semi-upright position, and then gently put the disassembled bicycle on top of her. It was a tight fit, but he was able to do so without scratching the car. He was mad at himself because he failed to properly research the interior of the Ferrari. He failed to discover ahead of time that the seat cannot lay fully flat. There was no time for self-chastisement. Time was of the essence. He would need a little luck to travel about a mile to where his car was parked. She had left the car running when she came to his aid. Before driving away, he studied the area where the abduction took place to see if there were any indications that the act took place in this exact spot. He saw no blood. No pieces of clothing. The entire act took place on the asphalt. No skid marks. He was satisfied that the area looked clean. He estimated he had been in the area less than five to seven minutes. He got in the car with his reluctant and unconscious passenger and left the Townsend road.

CHAPTER 10

The few moments driving back to his car were nerve-racking. He had just completed the part of the abduction that he considered the scariest. If someone had accidentally or unexpectedly come up to the scene, he really had no contingency plan to fall back on other than to just run. He often thought about that possibility, but finally decided it was a risk he would take. He glanced in the rearview mirror. No cars. The frontage road was void of any activity. As he pulled into the makeshift parking lot at the trailhead, he checked his watch and was pleased that he was within the time frame he had set for being this far along. He was on schedule.

The cumbersome part was now at hand. He had parked the Ferrari close to his car. He left enough room for him to transfer the limp and seemingly lifeless body of Chrystal from one car to the other. He anticipated that she would weigh about 115 pounds. He learned quickly that it was not so easy. Definitely not like lifting a sack of cement or bench pressing a similar weight at the gym. Her head was looking upward and was moving left and right like a bobblehead doll. Her arms and legs were dangling and flopping about. As he carried her to his car, she seemed to bend at the waist so that her shoulders slumped toward the ground, and her knees from the waist down had a similar inclination. It was awkward. Before he actually placed her in his car, he placed her hands on the steering wheel of the Ferrari and on the door handle of the driver's side. He made sure that his gloved hands did not smudge any of her prints. He also put the car keys in the console. Chris had adjusted the passenger seat so that she would be lying down and not easily seen by someone glancing at his car on the highway. He gently placed a blanket over her. Once he had her in place, he paused and looked down at her. Despite what she had just gone through, she looked fantastic. No time for admiration. He was on a schedule and had to keep moving.

Chris constantly checked the area to see if any early morning hikers, cars, or walkers could be seen. Nobody. So far so good. It was now time to police the area before leaving. If his pulse were to be taken at that very moment, it would be beating as fast as that of a beautiful, hyper, hummingbird. It felt like his shirt was actually moving in and out with each beat. He still had several things to do before he could leave. Everything was still quiet. No people. He moved his car the short distance of approximately twenty yards to the surface street. As he got out of his car, he froze. He heard a sound in the distance. He scanned the entrance road and the frontage road and he could not see anything or anybody. He stood still. A sigh of relief when he saw a helicopter that was flying very high off in the distance. The rhythmic chopping of the blades matched his heartbeat, only louder.

Chris walked back to where the transfer of Chrystal from one car to the other took place. Her shoes were stuffed in his waistband. He picked up the small tree branch he had earlier tossed on the ground. Now on his hands and knees, he moved backward and away from the parked Ferrari. He imprinted the soles of the shoes in the dirt and tried to gauge the distance of a step. He moved in the direction of the hiking trail. He stopped at a small grassy area that was partially covered with leaves that abutted the street. He was satisfied that he had made it appear as if she had started walking toward the trailhead. He walked from the road toward Chrystal's car. Once there, he started walking backward gently moved the branch across the dirt erasing his car's tire marks as well as his footsteps. He tried to make sure that the erasure and disturbance of the dirt did not look too unnatural. He did not want it to look like a Japanese Zen garden. His plan was to ensure shoe or tire prints were not discernible. He was satisfied that he had done everything he planned, and now it was time to head north on the PCH and complete the mission.

In the right lane of the northbound freeway, he drove at the speed limit. His hands were on the steering wheel in the "three and nine position," just like the driving manual recommended. His eyes darted from the side mirrors to the rearview mirror constantly. The traffic going south was heavy. It was a work day, and it was the usual commute grind that Los Angeles drivers endured daily. Northbound traffic was light. He looked at his watch and did a quick calculation of how much time had elapsed since the first application of chloroform was forced on Chrystal's face. He figured it has been at least twenty to twenty-five minutes. He was becoming concerned because it can start losing its effect after fifteen minutes or so, depending on the individual. Right on cue, Chrystal started to wiggle and twitch. He was ready for her to start coming out of the forced sleep. He removed the chloroform-soaked bandana from the satchel and placed it over her face. Once again she slipped back to an unconscious state and remained calm. The drive was uneventful, and he was now approaching the Port Hueneme turnoff. He couldn't resist the urge to touch this beautiful specimen of femininity just twelve inches away. He gently moved his fingertips across her face. Lightly following the contour of her cheeks, her forehead, her closed eyelids, the perfectly shaped nose, her neck, and then he eased his hand down on the blanket that covered her and put it on her breast. He quickly removed his hand. He was so excited. The entrance to the storage units rented by boat owners were just a few yards away.

He had to keep his wits about him and stay focused. After entering the storage area, he parked his Camry in such a manner that the passenger door was as close as possible to the entrance of his unit. Once again, he looked at his watch. Approximately forty to forty-five minutes had passed between the disassembly his bicycle and his arrival at the storage shed. He was pleased with his work so far. "I'm on time," he murmured to himself.

He raced through the combination lock with the correct numbers, but the lock failed to open. He couldn't believe it. He tried the numbers again and the lock popped open. He must have been nervous because he had circled the face of the lock one too many turns. He told himself to calm down. He took his own advice and slowed down. With the storage door now open, he carefully looked to see if anyone was within sight. Seeing no one, he quickly and firmly carried Chrystal through the door and placed her gently on the spinnaker sail he had bought and laid on the floor the previous evening. The chloroform was still doing its job. He shut the door but did not lock it. He moved his car to the marina parking area that was just a few yards away, but he could still see the storage locker. He doubled-checked to make sure there was nothing in the car except the pink slip (bill of sale) that he had removed from the glove compartment and placed on the passenger's seat. The buyer for the car would be there to finish the cash-only transaction of ownership at nine o'clock. Everything was still going smoothly. It was time for the next matter of business.

Still within sight of his storage locker, he picked up one of the flatbed push carts that were stored near the main entrance of the marina dock and brought it back to his storage locker. Boat owners are constantly moving items back and forth from their boats, so it's a common sight in the boating world to see people loading or unloading items from their boats. Before the final push to get the sail and Chrystal on his boat, he had to complete the car transaction. He calculated that he still had about fifteen minutes before the prearranged meeting with the buyer. In an abundance of caution, he once again applied a minimal amount of chloroform to Chrystal. He then carefully started rolling the sail over her body in such a way that she could not be seen. If anyone should happen to see him pushing the cart toward his boat, they wouldn't think anything of it. Chris then placed his trophy on the cart and secured her and the sail to the cart with bungee cords. Once again, he left the locker to consummate the car sale. Chris got his cash from the buyer, and the new owner now owned a Camry.

Before pushing his precious cargo away from the locker, he scanned the dock and the boats in their respective slips. Since it was a Tuesday and fairly early, there weren't any. He noted some owners at a distance, far enough away that it would be very unlikely that they would pay any attention to him. He placed both hands on the cart handle and started walking. He was so proud of himself as he confidently walked past the tethered boats. He counted that there were eight more boats to go until he reached his sailboat, and then said to himself, "I have done it." He took another step. Now seven boats to go. Then he heard a voice say, "Hi, Chris." He turned his head to see who had called his name. It was a friend of his parents' that he had known since he was a little boy.

"Oh, hi Mrs. Perkins."

"I just heard that you are getting ready to go on a long and extended sail. What's your destination?"

"I'm not really sure. I'm thinking about Alaska for starters, and then who knows." He glanced down at the spinnaker, hoping there would be no movement.

"Be safe, Chris. You are a good sailor. I'm sure your parents would be proud of you."

"I will, Mrs. Perkins," he shouted back to her. *No*, he thought, *my parents would be ashamed of me.* "I'll send you a postcard."

Without being rude, he slowly edged toward his boat. *Just five steps. Four, three, two...* And then he was boat side. He waved back to Mrs. Perkins and then turned his attention to hoisting the sail from the cart, along with the 110 pounds of beautiful and sexy woman who was protected like a future butterfly, safe in her cocoon, sound asleep.

It had now been roughly less than two hours since he partially choked out Chrystal, and he was now untying the lines that secured the boat to the dock in preparation to set sail. With the last line now on the deck, he slowly and cautiously eased away from his boat slip. *Au revoir,* Point Hueneme.

CHAPTER 11

There was a warm wind drifting down the California coastline. There was not enough wind to capture, so the sails would not be unfurled. Chris activated his thirty-five horsepower Johnson engine, and the prop spun into action. The speed would be slow so that the waves would be just ripples. Moderate to fast speed is not acceptable in the tranquil waters of marinas. The bow of the *Columbia* was pointed southwest as it distanced itself from the dock. He really had had no time to address how he was going to start the adventure of enjoying the fruits of his labors with the beautiful and physical body now below in the cabin. Of all the strange things to flash through his mind, as he stared at the horizon, was a flashback to when he was thirteen.

He reflected about an experience at a YMCA social mixer. He in seventh grade and very uncomfortable around girls. "Which still persists to this day," he reminded himself. He had gone to a dance and he remembered how hard the host tried to get the boys to dance. With some persuasion, the host cajoled one boy to get out on the dance floor. It was an ice breaker. Once the boy went out on the dance floor, others eventually followed. The "first move" was made and other activities followed.

The events of today were on a much more serious and grander scale. *How do I start with Chrystal?* He wasn't sure, but one way or another his lust would be fulfilled. As he was in this reflective mood, he thought he heard sounds of "his lady" moving about and mumbling incoherently below. He checked on her and noted that she was slowly coming out of the chloroform-induced state. He returned his attention to the helm to ensure he was on the course he had set. He wanted to get as far away from the California coast as quickly as possible. He had calculated that at five to six knots, he could be thirty to forty miles off shore in six hours, depending on the wind. So far the wind was cooperating. It was his calculation that the Townsend family would not suspect that anything was amiss until mid to late afternoon.

As the coastline faded away and the Malibu mountains started losing their definition, he started to become nervous about how he'd explain what he expected of Chrystal and the consequences if she did not acquiesce. He walked to the door of the belowdecks and stopped on the first step. He noted that she had started to stretch and twist her shoulders, and he thought he saw one of her eyes start to flutter as it tried to open. At that instant, he felt like a paratrooper on his first mission. He was now at the front of the line with the airplane door open. He was waiting for the jump master to yell *jump.* There was no turning back. Either jump or be pushed out of the plane. "Okay, here goes," he murmured to himself as he descended the seven steps and nervously eased into the cabin to face his "moment of truth."

Like all sailboats, the cabin was quite small. The only time a sense of space could be felt was topside. Chris sat on the edge of a wood-framed couch that could be converted into a bed. There was also a small amount of room for storage. Every inch of space in the *Columbia* was important. He was now less than two feet from Chrystal. He waited. Her eyes slowly opened. She looked to her left and then back to the right. It was obvious that she was confused. She still had not seen the man staring at her every move. She felt a sensation of movement. It was rhythmic. Left, right, then up, then slowly back down. Her mind was starting to click. It flashed back to a hurt man on the road. She had stopped to help. Then she was forcefully grabbed and something had made it hard to breathe. She was being choked. *Am I in a hospital? What has happened?* Then like in a bad dream that is so frightening, when you wake up, you are relieved that it was just a dream. In her semi-confused state, she turned her head and looked into the face of the man who had choked her. Her confusion turned to fright. She didn't scream. It was as if fright had taken away her ability to do so. Anyhow, who would hear her? She felt like a deer in the middle of a road, just standing there and staring at the headlights. Unwilling or unable to move. *Danger is here and now.* She quickly calculated that something sinister had happened, and she was fearful of what that might be. Her eyes quickly scanned the cabin. It was obvious that she was on a boat and at sea. The man continued to stare at her. He was nonverbal. She felt like a specimen being analyzed by a scientist, and he was fixated about what he saw under the lens of his microscope. *Am I alright?*

Have I been raped? Am I hurt? Thought after thought raced through her mind. The muted man was starting to look more and more sinister to her. She sat up and did a quick inventory of her body and clothes. She did not see anything untoward. Frightened and confused, she felt that she must talk to this stranger to try and understand what has happened. *Why am I here? What is this all about?* She turned to face the man who was just an arm's reach away.

"Please tell me why I'm here." *Who are you?* "Talk to me," Chrystal said in a controlled voice that masked her fear. Chris, who was conflicted himself and not quite sure how he was going to respond, knew that after a culmination of months of planning it was now time to tell her what would need to take place if she wanted to live.

"You will not like what I am about to tell you, but what you like or dislike doesn't matter to me. You are my possession. You will do as requested or the consequences will be severe." Chris is pleased with his hard-line choice of introductory words and the implied threat. After the harsh and scary comments, he paused and let his eyes focus on her ankles and slowly move up from there to her shapely legs and inner thighs. He paused at that point before continuing the visual journey to her breasts, where he lingered. He was obviously becoming aroused. He was about to reach over to her and touch her face and hair, but stopped because she was now becoming hysterical.

She was sobbing heavily and tears were cascading down her high cheekbones. Her beautiful facial coloring was turning ashen with fear. She was trembling. Chrystal slumped over and buried her face in the bed. She could not stop her body from the muscular convulsions taking place. Chris decided to wait before he spoke to her again.

"Before I go topside, I want you to think about what I told you. Pull yourself together. There is no place to go. No one to help you. You're smart. Figure out how you want to act. I'll talk to you after you compose yourself." He walked up the seven steps out of the cabin to the helm where he scanned the horizon. The only thing he saw was the vastness of the ocean. He stood at the helm with both hands on the wheel and gently adjusted his course. He reflected on what had just taken place.

The panting, the sobbing, the rhythm of her gasps for air were in harmony with the hypnotic swaying of the boat. Very slowly and with great effort, Chrystal started taking small but fairly deep breaths of the ocean air and forced herself to become calm enough to try and make sense of what obviously was a serious, dangerous, and possibly a life-threatening situation. She could not get the words *you are my possession* out of her mind. The meaning of those words were ominous. It did not take her long to realize that her survival depended upon her intellectual and mental capacity to adjust and try to deal with whatever lay ahead. She got up off the bed and wiggled and twisted into the cramped toilet area. She gasped when she looked at herself in the under-sized mirror. The boat was pitching and swaying, so she had to steady herself with one hand holding on to the spigot and the other hand cleaning her face and readjusting her beautiful blond hair that was now twisted and matted. Traces of where the tears left lines on her cheeks, similar to the trail left by snails as they move from place to place. Her eyes were flushed rose red. There was just a trace of white in her corneas showing. She dabbed away the almost microscopic tears from her lashes. As she stared at herself, she noted the bruise on her neck, which she deduced was from the chokehold that occurred when she was kidnapped. As she stared into the mirror, she slowly turned her head from side to side thinking that she looked like hell. "But what the hell," she whispered to the person in front of her, and murmured, "It's time to face the monster who threatens my very existence." She inched herself out of the toilet and headed for the seven steps that would lead her topside. Before she placed her foot on step one, she reminded herself, "Do not be hostile. Stay calm. Do not upset him. Be smart. Okay, here goes."

CHAPTER 12

There was a gentle breeze coming out of the south, and Chris kept the bow into the wind and on a southern track that required an occasional westward tack. It was a warm day, and there was not a single cloud in the azure sky. A picture-perfect day.

The *Columbia* was slicing through the calm sea at a leisurely two knots. He really didn't care about the speed. His only immediate goal was to leave California in his wake, which was occurring without a hitch. He felt terrific. As he was mentally congratulating himself on what he had achieved during this Tuesday, he glanced at his watch and noted the time. It was almost noon. He felt safe and secure. Time was no longer a factor. He rested his hands on the helm and stared at the bow as it gently bobbed up and down as it kissed the oncoming morning wind. It was hypnotic. He was getting himself aroused as he anticipated what he planned to do next with the sexy and beautiful woman who was just a few feet away. His fantasy was broken when he heard footsteps belowdecks that were caused by Chrystal coming up the stairwell. She was now fewer than two armlengths away. He could easily touch her. He planned to do just that, and soon.

She sat on a cushion, crossed her perfectly shaped legs, then faced him and spoke. "I have calmed down now, and need to know what is going to happen. I'm not afraid, I just need to know. Please tell me." She was terrified, but hoped it didn't show. Chris made the necessary adjustment to have the ship automatically maintain the desired course, then faced Chrystal.

"I most certainly will tell you, Chrystal, but first I want to go over a few facts with you, which I am sure will influence how you handle the situation that is your new reality. Let me explain to you why it is in your best interest not to resist my wishes and demands. I believe that I have completed a perfect abduction that will ensure that I will never be suspected or discovered." He then went on to outline the salient facts of how he planned and executed the kidnapping.

"One. As a barista at the coffee shop, I saw you for the first time. I was enraptured by your beauty. You became an obsession. The more I saw you, the idea of how to do something about my lust for you grew. On the brief occasions when you entered the store, I never waited on you. I never said anything to any of the staff about you. No one knew anything of my feelings about you.

"Two. I started planning on how to cope with my fantasy that was spiraling out of control. I quit my job at Starbucks. I sold the family home. I lived full-time on my boat. For several days, I parked my car in the parking lot while you went to the spa four days a week. I made sure there were no security cameras. I parked by a dumpster far from the spa entrance and took pictures of you from a distance with my telescopic lens. The photos fueled my obsession for you. I am positive that no one saw me photographing you.

"Three. I researched where you live and the surrounding area with a drone. I also cataloged the approximate times you left the house to go to the spa, and I studied the private road to your estate.

"Four. Once I had your time patterns down pat, I staged the fake bicycle accident and the abduction, which took less than five minutes. You stopped your car gradually to help me. There are no skid marks. I policed the area to ensure there was no evidence of our brief struggle. No one saw what took place.

"Five. We returned to the hiking trail where I had parked my car. After transferring you from your car to mine, I made sure that the only prints on your car were yours. I moved my car to the asphalt and returned to your car. I then used your shoes to embed some prints in the dirt leading to the hiking trail. I gently erased my footprints and tire markings. No one saw any of the activity that took place.

"Six. While you were unconscious, I drove to my rented storage space. I placed you in a large sail that I had acquired just for the purpose of moving you from the storage area to my boat. I rolled you up inside the sail, placed you on a push cart, and moved you to the boat. No one was aware of what was taking place.

"Seven. So, in less than a couple of hours, we pushed off from the dock and headed for the open sea. No one will be concerned or suspicious about you for several hours, and by then, California will be many miles away."

While Chris was confident and proud of the way he reviewed this morning's activities, Chrystal's mental and physical being was in turmoil. He had made it a point to start each poignant stage of his achievement by saying numbering them from one to seven. With each number he mentioned, she felt like how the Chinese tortured people by using *lingchi*, also known as death by a thousand cuts—small razor-like cuts to the body that caused the person to have a lingering and slow death. Each number he spoke was a razor slash. Prior to saying anything, she quickly calculated the immense danger and uncertainty of the moment. *This guy has kidnapped me and might get away with it. I have to get time on my side if I want to survive.* As she contemplated what to say or do, she was interrupted by Chris.

"Okay, I have made it fairly clear of what I expect. What do you have to say?" He was exuding male superiority and dominance as he spoke. Chrystal perceived that he was getting fidgety and perhaps aroused. *Say something. Be smart*, she kept saying over and over to herself.

Masking her fears and anxiety, she made some feminine gestures and movements that suggested she was not intimidated by the forced physical and sexual occurrences that were about to take place. She erased all signs of worry and doubt the best she could and looked up at him. With a hint of allure and mystique, she flipped back a wisp of her blond hair and said, "Why don't we start this adventure with you telling me your name?"

"My name is Chris, and I certainly know your name."

"Well Chris, I guess I should be, and maybe I am, flattered that you are so impressed with me that you went through such an effort to bring us together to start this adventure."

"Impressed is not the word. Obsessed is more like it," Chris responded. "It's time for us to go below and let me enjoy every inch of your body. I hope you will not be difficult because as you can see, there is no one who can help you out but yourself."

With softness of an angel she said, "I will not be difficult. I will do everything I can to get to know you, and hopefully we will get along just fine.

I'd like to have a few moments below to prepare for what lies ahead. Is that agreeable to you?"

"Of course, but don't keep me waiting too long," he said. He was so impressed with how things were working out. Things were going better than he could possibly have hoped for. Chrystal unfolded her long and beautifully shaped legs and slowly got up from the cushion. With the air of a high fashion model, she walked past Chris who slightly grazed her derrière (another razor slash) as she walked by and descend into the dreaded cabin where the psychological cuts and slashes would multiply.

Now alone, he scanned the ocean in every direction and was pleased to note that there was not a single thing to see, just as he expected. No helicopters, no coast guard patrol boats, nothing. As he continued to stare at the vastness of the ocean, a voice from the cabin below called out, "Chris."

CHAPTER 13

As Chris started his descent into the cabin, he paused for a brief instant as he heard soft music wafting up the airways drifting in his direction. He took another step and paused once again. He felt a pleasant feeling of euphoria and lightheadedness as he saw Chrystal lying on the bed with a sheet that partially covered her body. It was arranged in such a manner that a portion of her firm breasts were exposed. He could visualize her nude body beneath the peek-a-boo sheet. The longer he looked at her, he got the impression that she might have discarded all of her clothes. As he was considering that possibility, Chrystal partially slipped the sheet lower and exposed enough of her body to confirm that she was indeed unclothed. He was beside himself with anticipation and excitement. Chrystal had a trace of a smile on her lips as she coquettishly invited him to come to her. There were no signs of drying tears lining her cheeks. She looked absolutely beautiful and sexy. She turned on her side and propped her head on her hand in such a way that both of her breasts were now partially exposed. As her head rested on her hand, she motioned with her index finger for him to enter the bed.

Momentarily, Chris felt stunned. He had never been with a woman and now that he had this magical moment. He felt awkward and inept, and even somewhat embarrassed as to how he should act and proceed.

Clumsily, he started removing the few items of clothing he was wearing. As he was doing so, Chrystal gave him a look that seemed to say "What are you waiting for?" Finally the awkwardness started to ebb, and he approached her and gently eased onto the bed. He wasn't sure if he should kiss her or just how to start this sexual journey. He started to kiss her and she gently moved his head aside and whispered to him, "Not now, later." He was not offended. Without any further delay, he entered Chrystal. Chris was ecstatic. Months of planning and execution of his plans had now come to fruition. After the climatic end there was no conversation. Both were silent. The sounds of the ocean lapping and bumping against the bow as it sliced through the calm seas seemed louder than usual. Chris did not know exactly what to say, and Chrystal offered nothing. It was an uncomfortable quietness. Chris removed himself from the small bed located in the bow and started to dress. He felt like a fool as he said, "Thank you." Chrystal smiled and said nothing. The boat captain, now dressed, bounded up the seven steps with the same spirit that someone might have when clicking their heels with happiness and delight. Chrystal buried her head in the pillow and sobbed.

Chrystal touched her eyes with the edge of the soiled and damp sheet to remove the tears that had accumulated as she reflected on what had just occurred. She looked down at the floor and shook her head back and forth thinking about her life. Just a few hours ago, her life was orderly and secure with unlimited opportunities, and now she was a sex object for a disturbed man and aboard a forty-one foot sailboat heading for the vastness of the Pacific Ocean. Destination unknown. She had quickly assessed that the slightest mishap could be fatal. She was now floating on the surface of what could be her burial site. As a result of her assessment, she recalled her mantra. *Be smart.* It was this thought process that encouraged her to remember to placate Chris as best as she could until hopefully she could extract herself from this life-threatening situation. One of the first and very hard decisions she had to make was to not discourage his sexual demands and have him continue to think of her as a special and beautiful woman. The sex act that just occurred was her first major concession to live up to her slogan of "be smart." Before today, she had had only one brief sexual encounter. It happened when she had attended a sorority and frat party in her junior year of college. The culmination of learning how to drink alcohol and being taken advantage of resulted in her first and only sexual involvement, until now. Ergo, the charade of being an experienced woman in that area just took place. She would try to give the impression that she looked forward to his romantic overtures. As far as she was concerned, what just happened was repulsive and disgusting. The razor cuts kept coming. "Enough reflection and contemplation," she murmured. "Time to face reality."

She yelled to Chris, "I'm going to take a shower."

He instantly responded. "Wait, I'll be right down." Chrystal waited. With a sheet wrapped around her body, she stood at the entrance to the diminutive bathroom door. There wasn't a trace of fear or anger on her face as she waited for the captain to appear. At least that was the appearance she wished for him to perceive. Inside, fear and anger were consuming her. He descended the stairs with the swagger of a conquering solider and gently touched her face with his hand. He told her that there were a lot of things about a boat she will have to learn. "There is no shower and all bathing is done by an occasional sponge bath. Note the word 'occasional.'"

"A what?" Chrystal asked.

"Every once in a while, like maybe three or four days, you can have a couple of quarts of water for bathing. Use it sparingly. Dip a washcloth in some of the water, lather the cloth with soap, and then wash yourself. Use the remainder of the water to rinse off the soap. You actually do not use a sponge. We cannot waste water, and I would love to give you your first bath."

"No thanks," she said. "I get the concept. Will you get me the water? I will make two quarts of water do the trick."

When Chris returned with her ration of water, he went on to explain that the boat only has storage for one hundred gallons of water, which he supplemented with several large bottles that increased the total amount of water to thirty gallons. "That's all we have until we drop anchor somewhere and we can get needed supplies."

Chrystal liked the words "anchor" and "we." Without showing any urgency or worry she casually asked, "Oh, any idea when or where that might be?"

Chris did not respond to her inquiry. As he was heading up the stairs, he yelled back to her, "Don't take too long, it looks like we are going to have a great sunset. Come join me."

The way Chris said join me for a sunset was like an invitation to a lovely way to spend some time together watching nature draw down the curtain for the day. A warm, inspirational, bonding time together. It would be nothing like that for Chrystal. As she visualized sitting with him looking seaward, it would be like viewing the endless mass of the sea as a potential cemetery. Still reeling and numb from what had happened to her today, she reflected on how many terrible things had happened, and there was still daylight.

Mumbling to the walls of the cabin, "I've been choked, kidnapped, drugged, manhandled, raped, and now I'm on a sailboat with a sex maniac sailing on the Pacific Ocean, destination unknown." What she really wanted to do was yell, scream, cry and have this nightmare end. Reality caught up with her internal spasm of emotionalism. She slowly dipped the soap-laden washcloth into her quart of warm water and applied it to her exquisite body and face, which was responsible for attracting this man to her and the events that had since transpired. The second quart of water was used to "sponge" off the first quart. Refreshed but depressed, she dressed and headed for the stairwell to watch *el sol* drop below the horizon. So, another day was now drawing to a close. Unfortunately, it also meant an evening in the double bed with the ship's captain.

CHAPTER 14

It was Friday morning. Chrystal opened her eyes very slowly. The first indicators of the start of a new day were coming into focus. The darkness of the cabin was giving way to the light of day four of her captivity. As she lay there reflecting on how she had to endure the physical demands of Chris last night, her thoughts were interrupted. The normal rocking of the boat was different. It felt like the sea was in a slow rolling pattern and the boat was slowly and gently being lifted up and down. The rise and dip of the boat was hardly noticeable. It was such a slow and deliberate motion that Chrystal became mesmerized by the boat's movement and she started to drift back to sleep. Before the final closure of her eyelids took place, she wondered why he wasn't wiggling around and trying to touch her or arouse her as was his usual style or intent every morning. *That's curious*, she thought. Chrystal slowly rolled over on her side and looked toward Chris's side of the bed. He was not there. The unusual behavior of the sea this morning and the absence of Chris's early morning antics were curious enough to motivate her to get out of bed. She eased out of bed and decided to go topside and see what's up.

Chrystal saw Chris at the bow of the boat noted he seemed to be gauging and studying something. He looked skyward and east and west repeatedly. She approached and in a cheerful and pleasant way, despite the fact that she loathed, despised, and hated him.

"Good morning, Chris. You are up a bit early, aren't you?"

"Hi, Chrystal. I'm trying to figure out what is going on with this weather."

"What do you mean?" she asked.

"The calmness of the ocean and the heat kicking up makes me wonder if we are in for a siege of the doldrums."

"The doldrums?"

"Let's have some morning coffee and I'll explain what that might mean for us."

"Okay. I'll go below and brew a couple of cups. I'll skimp on the amount of water I use." As Chrystal left the bow, she carefully walked to midship, holding onto the stainless steel guide lines to ensure she did not trip or fall. Chris enjoyed watching her depart. If he were an artist, he would ensure that her beauty and grace would be captured on canvas. Different scenes and images entered his mind. One for sure would be a nude painting. He momentarily lost his train of thought about the weather as he digressed about the treasure that he now possessed and enjoyed every second of every day. His infatuation with thoughts of sex and affection about Chrystal were interrupted when she yelled, "Coffee's ready!" His brain switched from the dreamy world of Chrystal and him to the serious and business side of two people on a sailboat that might have to rely on each other as they face the potential challenges of a sea that can be pleasant and enjoyable as well as dangerous and deadly.

Now settled underneath a tarp that covered the cockpit area, they sat on cushions facing each other. The mainsail and the jib caught what little breeze possible that was coming out of the north as they sailed on a straight southern course. The autopilot was locked in place so there was no reason to alter their course by tacking. Even though the day was slowly warming up, the hot coffee hit the spot. Chrystal sat patiently waiting for Chris to speak. This would be the first time he had actually set time aside to engage in a talk with her. She was hopeful she could use this opportunity to gain some idea of what lay ahead. She crossed her legs underneath her body, sipped her coffee, and waited.

"Where do I want to start?" he said as he gazed at the horizon for a few seconds. He turned to face Chrystal and said, "Look, I make no apologies for what has happened and I'm glad I did what I did, whether you like it or not. If you want live and survive, you will need to make some major changes in your attitude and acceptance of your situation." Chrystal squirmed on the cushion and slowly adjusted her position, keeping her eyes on Chris's face as she waited for whatever was to come next. His emphasis on certain words and his tone of voice was scaring her. She tried to look calm and attentive, but inside she was in turmoil. His face was hard and his eyes had a penetrating and menacing look as he looked into her eyes. There was no warmth or comfort in his face or demeanor.

"I enjoy and look forward to the sex I have with you, which I will continue to have, but it's time that you adopt another role for me and that is you have to become a shipmate, not just a sex mate. It's necessary for your survival, and to some extent, mine. My nautical instincts and background have heightened my concern that in a few days we may have some unpredictable and difficult weather ahead. I could change the word 'difficult' for 'dangerous.'" He hit the pause button on his conversation and turned his attention to his cooling cup of coffee. Slowly, methodically, he started stirring his spoon around and around as he seemed to be contemplating what to say next. It was quiet. Chrystal was seething inside. He used a phrase that made her almost explode and unleash a torrid of hate-filled things and thoughts to this young and confused fool. Referring to her as "sex mate" was nauseous to the extreme. Trying to control herself, she blankly looked to the sea. She didn't see or feel the softness of the gentle water caressing the boat and nudging it along; the deep blue expanse of the ocean with its awe inspiring beauty; the intoxicating fragrance of the sea. Instead she wondered how many people over the millennia had perished and were permanent denizens of the sea. Her mind drifted. It was like looking at cloud formations.

Using your imagination, you might see a smiling face or a giraffe with his long legs and neck. Those are pleasant reflections. *If I kill this fool, then what?* she asks herself. That thought had entered her mind after a few hours at sea after realizing how desperate her situation was and might become. She quickly dismissed that idea. Still gazing at the ocean, her imagination conjured up an image that was anything but pleasant. She saw grey mounds, lots of them, headstones for those who had died at sea. The water was no longer blue, it was turning grey. She shivered. The sound of a spoon hitting the inside of a coffee cup stopped. Chrystal passively looked at Chris, waiting. *What's next?* He broke the silence by saying, "Chrystal, I want to go over the term I used, "shipmate," with you. Situations could develop where our lives depend on us working together. Are you on board with that?"

"Of course, let's get started," she replied.

CHAPTER 15

"When you saw me on the bow studying the weather patterns, I started worrying if we might be in store for a major weather change. The dreaded doldrums." He went on to explain (not in detail) what that could mean to them in the days, possibly weeks ahead. Continuing on as if he were talking to a classroom of students with an interest in sailing, he got to the bottom line first. "There is little to zero wind. You can be dead in the water. You are stuck. It is a condition that can be followed by thunderstorms and nasty sea conditions as a byproduct. The area is considered one of the most dangerous in the world for boats that rely on the wind for movement." Chrystal temporarily put aside her thinking about her hatred and dislike of the twenty-two-year-old professor now lecturing in the cockpit area, one hand on the helm, the other rubbing his chin in deep thought, thinking what to say next. He had her attention. She also learned that her prior conception of the "doldrums" didn't relate to only someone who was feeling blue or down in the dumps. She had never put a nautical spin on the phrase. He stopped talking and went forward to sheet the jib.

After returning to the "classroom," he told her that he felt that this morning's calm sea was probably just an aberration. He went on to explain that historically, the doldrums occur near the equator where the strong north and south winds collide. The hot, scorching sun over the area where the winds collide causes the air to go straight up, not horizontally. The sea loses the wind and is dead calm. This is frequently followed by strong storms and hurricanes. Chris could see that the only student in attendance looked seriously concerned. "So Chrystal, we need to be prepared. We will not be close to the equator for at least ten days or more, depending on the wind. This is a large sailboat and it might be impossible for me to handle the boat alone under extreme weather conditions." To reassure and ease her apparent fright, he advised her that he had prepared for unexpected situations and problems. "Don't be scared. We can handle most contingencies. We just have to be mentally and physically organized in times of stress and emergencies. So, with that said, let's take a walk around the ship and I'll go over some things with you."

He called it "the ship," but she considered it a floating prison cell. The instructive tour of the floating penitentiary would have been boring for her under normal conditions, but with the frightening preamble about the doldrums, she did pay attention. She temporally set aside her loathing of Chris and recognized the potential that learning about the boat, might, or could, fit in with her burning and intense desire to survive.

The sea was still calm, which meant that the educational stroll was accomplished without many interruptions. Chrystal had always been a fast learner, so she did not have a difficult time learning and understanding new terms and the various functions of the equipment. New words would soon become a part of her daily vocabulary. So on this particular educational stroll, the words started to evolve. Some of them would include jib; sheeting the sails; call guide lines, "lines," not rope; halyard; autopilot; bilge; gallery; cockpit. It was a growing list, but she had no doubt that she would learn them and their importance in the operation of the boat. There were two items that Chris mentioned that really had an impact on her. Because he expected severe weather before they passed through the equator, he spent some time on where the tether safety lines were located and how to engage them. The second point he brought up was the flying of the American flag. It wasn't comforting how he phrased it. "If it looks hopeless and desperate, we will fly the flag upside down. It is internationally recognized by the boating world as a serious problem aboard."

While Chris was telling her about the boat, he made one comment that was like approaching an accident on the freeway and the ambulance and police cars' red lights are flashing. Warning lights. When he mentioned the time frame of ten days or more before they approach the equator, she swallowed hard but with difficulty.

After talking a lot about technical words and terms, he suggested to Chrystal that she do a close inventory of the galley and living area. He explained that many things that are still in some of the cupboards and storage areas belonged to his parents. "My parents took many long sailing trips so they accumulated all sorts of gear and equipment that I just didn't want to get rid of. You might find things that will interest you. If so, help yourself. While you are doing that, I will do some maintenance on the boat."

Once below deck, Chrystal started studying the area with a heightened interest. She constantly thought about how, when, or if, she could gain her freedom and get out of this horrible, scary, and frightening mess. Maybe she might come upon something or get an idea of what she could do by exploring every nook and cranny of the galley. Like most boats, every inch of space is important so she was motivated to get to work. She removed the cushions from all the sitting areas, then started removing items that had been stored beneath them. For the most part, the items were things you would expect to find. Extra pillows and bedding, tools, some canned goods, and foul weather clothes, which she carefully set aside for the moment. She discovered that his mother had stored some of her clothing as well as a plastic pouch with some cosmetics that she must have long ago forgotten about. The immediate thought came to her mind that finally she could have something else to wear. As she was tugging and pulling his mother's personal items closer to her, something else came into view. It was an extra flare gun. She knew it was an extra because in Chris's orientation class, he pointed out a flare gun and explained how it worked. She carefully replaced the gun and placed a variety of items on top of it. She did not know if the gun would be of any value to her at a later date, but then again, it might.

Continuing with her search of various compartments, she found one that was full of things to occupy one's time on long sailing trips. There were puzzles, novels, books on crocheting, needle point, knitting, yarn, some nettles, and a fairly large bag of wine corks. She thought that was unusual, but then she remembered the cork bulletin board by the propane stove. She thought it was a clever idea. She saw these various items as an omen of what lay ahead. Lots and lots of downtime. Boredom. The scavenger hunt was interrupted by a call from Chris for her to come topside and help sheet the sails and learn how to cleat lines. The wind was picking up, and he wanted to use it to their advantage.

Before going topside, she tried on some of his mother's clothes. She selected a tank top and shorts that would probably be stylish for most middle age women. She could have cared less how she looked. Not her style, but different and clean. It made her feel good, even in this dire situation. It was time to go topside. Chris was waiting for her in the cockpit area. As she was taking her last step and about to enter the area, Chris said, "Hold it. Stop right there." He wanted to just look at her, frozen in time for a few seconds. Even in his mom's clothes she looked terrific. "Wow, you look great. You could wear anything and look fantastic." Most unwelcome compliments as far as she was concerned. Her reply was not one of appreciation, but a rather icy "What do you want me to do?"

The captivity and atmosphere was starting to have a routine feel. Chrystal's outward signs of fear were more hidden and internalized. She was cautious not to anger her hated abductor because he obviously was capable of physically harming her. If he snapped, she could be tossed overboard and become food for the sharks. To keep her sanity and cope with the situation she needed something to do that would keep her busy mentally and physically. One thing she decided as a must was that she had to stay in the best physical shape. If somehow an opportunity to escape should ever occur, being in good condition might be required. She approached Chris with the idea that if possible and if it was safe enough could she swim as often as possible. She told him she was a poor swimmer but, "You want me to keep my shape, don't you?" She knew he would agree to her question, and he did. On the mental side of the equation, she had to learn her job as a neophyte sailor on the boat and at the same time get involved in some craft projects. She liked what his mom did with the creativity of using the corks for useful as well as decorative purposes. Maybe she'd give that a try. Like her mom, she loved puzzles. Doing puzzles would also give her a feeling of contact with her mom whom she missed terribly. So today, as they inched along to the equator, she had settled on her agenda. Stay fit. Crafts. Be a good sailor. Survive.

CHAPTER 16

The sheriff for the Malibu area said good morning to his top investigators who met with him almost daily about the Townsend case. Three weeks had passed since the disappearance of Chrystal Townsend. Her father had been a big supporter in his reelection and often called him several times a day for updates. So far, he had been unable to give him any encouraging news. Today's meeting was, once again, to review the case in detail.

Directing his attention to the lead detective, the sheriff asked him to go over what they had done to date. He responded by saying that he would generalize the investigation to date and give specifics on any portion if required.

"The woman had been missing for several hours before it was reported to the department. Close to twelve hours had passed. The location of the car wasn't discovered until the next day. It was parked near the trail that hikers use when they enter the Santa Monica mountains. The car was checked by forensics. They found nothing helpful for us. The only fingerprints in or on the car belonged to Townsend. No pieces of clothing, hair follicles, et cetera were detected. During the search of the car her car keys were found, which suggests she had every intention to return to the car after a hike. Pure speculation. What is believed to be her footprints were found walking in the direction of the mountain trail. No other footprints were found near the car. The initial focus was to search all the trails to see if she could be found. A large number of volunteers helped in the search for several days. We used the helicopter on three different occasions.

"As of today, we really don't know if she entered the mountains, or if she did, what might have occurred. There are reports of mountain lions that roam the area we searched. We factored that into our search as well. We interviewed scores of people looking for useful information. We concentrated on areas that she is known to frequent. We did not get any leads or helpful information.

We also checked security cameras in areas where she visits for one reason or another. We did not observe anything that looked suspicious to us. We did not uncover any info about problems with ex boyfriends. Everything in that area was normal. No spurned boyfriends. No love triangles. The volunteers posted missing person signs all over the Malibu and Santa Monica areas. The signage hasn't been helpful to date.

"There has been one troubling aspect of the investigation that has bothered all of us working this case. We were told by many of her friends and family that she is a very organized person, and it surprised most of them that she failed to arrive at the spa as she does every Tuesday. They feel—and we tend to agree—there is an incongruity of taking a hike instead of her usual spa commitment on the day she disappeared. Concluding this briefing this morning, it should be mentioned that at no time did we eliminate the possibility that her disappearance could have been deliberate. This possibility was mentioned frequently to her friends and family. Not a single person believed that was possible. Then again, you really don't know for sure. That concludes our report as of today."

"Well, when I called the Townsend family with this latest update, I had hoped to give them some encouraging news, but just doesn't seem to be the case. When I talked with them yesterday, they told me that the two prestigious private investigation firms they hired had also hit a brick wall in their efforts to find his daughter. So, I want you keep the file open. Keep me posted on the status of the case. Good luck. That'll do it for now."

"Good morning, sheriff. Anything new?" asked Chrystal's dad.

"No, I'm afraid not."

"Okay, keep your guys on the case and give me a call tomorrow. Don't give up. I don't want this to become a cold case. Thanks for the update."

"Okay, I'll call you in a day or so—or sooner, if something of importance develops. I have my best guys on this case and in this instance the term 'cold case' doesn't exist for them." The sheriff hit the off button on his phone and was starting to have doubts if any new developments would occur.

CHAPTER 17

Now approaching several weeks at sea, both Chris and Chrystal had developed daily patterns of how they spent their time. Today started out like most of the days did. When not helping Chris with some chore on the boat, she spent time doing crafts. She taught herself how to crochet and was slowly using up the yarn Chris's mom left on the boat. She loved the challenge of making decorative items from bindles of cork that were also left on the boat. Especially since she had no glue. She trimmed the pieces of cork and then used fish line or thread to bind the size and shapes of items she created. So far she had crafted a small bulletin board that she hung in the area they used for writing and reading. In a more creative and inventive mode, she gathered some materials she found and shaped two large stingrays. Using some discarded rubber she found, she sliced the cork vertically and then attached the sliced cork to some rather old and stiff rubber. Just to give it an artistic flair, she made exaggerated tails. She was particularly proud of the matching stingrays that now hung over the small butane stove. This morning, sitting under the tarp that covered the cockpit area, she was concentrating on her crochet work. As she was slipping the needle under the yarn for the next stitch, she heard Chris in the water supply area. He had a concerned look on his face. Chrystal put down the project and within a few steps was by his side. "Is something wrong?" she asked. He didn't respond. She had noticed that he had been becoming more and more moody lately. She did not pursue her inquiry and returned to the cockpit area.

During the past weeks, Chrystal had been noticing a definite change in Chris's mental state, and it was making her worried and nervous. While trying to speculate why his personality and behavior were going through these changes, she felt an involuntary muscle spasm throughout her body. She shivered. It was possible that the enormity of what he had done was sinking in and what to do about it was occupying his mind and he did not like how it could turn out. As she speculated, she did a transference of positions. Trying to think like he might, she came up with a frightening conclusion. *If he's right, he will not be caught, unless I somehow live or escape and tell what really happened. To eliminate that possibility, he will have to kill me.* She felt very vulnerable and helpless as she came to that conclusion. She had spent days staring at the ocean thinking about her situation, and the only action she could think of to avoid her own death was to kill him. Of course, she did not know if she had the wherewithal to follow through on such an act. She doubted it. As she had said to herself countless times, *then what?* A small watercraft floating in a vast ocean with virtually no chance of being found. So, contemplating and rejecting most ideas that she thought of many, many times, she started to develop a new thought that might stall and give her additional time to hopefully figure out something to get her out of this horrible situation. At least until they pass through the equator. She will start working on her new idea right away. (The old idea that was with her every single second was *escape*.)

Chrystal eased out from the shade of the tarp and walked over to the water storage area. It looked like Chris was actually measuring how much water they had on hand. He paid little attention to her presence. "Chris, I am worried about how much help I can be if we are hit with a major storm as we approach the equator. You have told me the odds are it could be difficult and dangerous. I want to be sure I can help you as much as I can to ensure that you will be as safe as possible for both our sake. What can I do to help us be prepared?" He seemed to be listening, but he didn't respond. So she added, "Is the weather changing? It feels like the wind is dying and it is getting kinda calm. Look, there are hardly any waves or ripples on the ocean." He continued to assess the water supply. She stood by.

"Chrystal, we have been at sea for close to a month, and I figure if we have averaged three knots a day, we are closing in on the distance from L.A. to the equator, which is over two thousand miles. As you noted, the wind is almost nonexistent. I think we are starting to see the start of the doldrums. We have to be careful in the days—I hope not weeks—ahead. Careful with our water supply and food. Also, if I have to use our engine from time to time to keep us moving south, I need to monitor how much gas I use. So, it's careful sailing for a while and a sparing use of critical supplies. Why don't you check the jib and mainsail and trim them so we can capture what little wind we can while I check the engine and gas tank."

Chrystal felt satisfied with her effort to place the importance of her presence on the boat and getting a slight shift in his mood from being sullen and withdrawn to alert and talkative. After checking the sails, she decided that today she would try her hand, once again, at fishing. Especially since he mentioned the food supply as something they needed to monitor. It was something real and positive to be doing. The days were long and mostly boring, and fishing was a good distraction. It also required a degree of concentration and therefore kept her mind occupied with the task at hand. She dropped the line aft of the boat and trolled the line as the boat barely moved in a southern direction. Her mind never stopped jumping from one topic to another as she scanned the water hoping to see something other than just the ocean. So, as she fixated her eyes on the sea and stared at it, her mind developed a philosophical thought. The ocean is never the same. It's like watching a campsite fire. Every fire is completely and always different. Today, as she stared blankly seaward, it occurred to her that the ocean isn't really changing at all. It is like looking a Claude Monet seascape painting. In her mind, it was the same every day. Nothing changed. Blue water, white or gray clouds, sun comes up, sun goes down, same for the moon, the stars were always, it seemed, fixed in place. Day after day, the cycle repeated itself. Just like the painting, it was the same every time you looked at it. *So*, she thought, *its changing but it isn't*. She was sick of looking at the sea. Chrystal started to slip into a depressive mental frame of mind when the fish line came alive. So did she. She reeled in a decently size red snapper. With it dangling and wiggling on the line, she showed Chris dinner for tonight as she walked to the galley.

Another day was winding down. Evening was descending over the almost microscopic dot in the ocean—the forty-one-foot *Columbia* sailboat. Chris and Chrystal were both topside and at opposite ends of the boat. Perhaps they were wondering what the other was thinking, or perhaps planning. There was one thing for sure, both were very much aware that a weather change was occurring. It was getting warmer and the sea was unusually quiet. Another long and sad day in the life of Chrystal Townsend was drawing to a close.

CHAPTER 18

Sunrise. It was already hot. The captain and his shipmate were slowly starting to wake up and face another day at sea. The only real bed on the ship was in the bow. It was the worst place to sleep when the waves increased in size and frequency. The bow would rise and then slap down to the sea with each up and down movement of the boat. It made movement and balance difficult. This morning, there really wasn't any movement. As both of them had anticipated and discussed, they must be nearing the equator more quickly than they had anticipated. As they lay there, neither one said anything as if to give the impression that they were still asleep. Because of the constant heat, Chris only slept in his boxer shorts. He slowly turned his body so he could see Chrystal. She was wearing a pair of shorts and a soiled tee shirt, and she was facing him on the small bed. He partially opened his eyes and looked at her. She was no longer the most absolutely beautiful woman who excited him and motivated him to abduct. He started assessing her from head to toe.

Her hair was always immaculate. Clean, with a sheen that highlighted the rich blond color of her hair that flowed and sparkled in the breeze. Now, it is all matted and unkempt. It reminded him of a mop that was hung up to dry and dangled in the sunlight. Scraggly and without form. When he looked at her face, he slowly moved his head from side to side suggesting disbelief in what he was looking at. Before her rapid weight loss, one of the highlights of her face was her high cheek bones. Now her face was so much thinner that the bones were beginning to become so pronounced that it made her look skeletal. Her facial skin reflected the damage of daily exposure to the wind and sun. A complexion that was once flawless and the coloring exquisite was now is dry in appearance. She had the beginning of a sore on her lip that was completely distracting from her once full and inviting lips. She had no makeup, so her lips were colorless and dry.

Continuing with his early morning evaluation of Chrystal, he could not see her breasts because of the stained tee shirt she was wearing. He knew from his forced sex (even though she never resisted, he knew she had no choice) with her that her breasts were not as firm and their size had changed, and not for the better. Of all her physical features, he felt like her long, shapely, well-tanned, and firm legs excited him the most. They were still long but not so shapely, and much thinner. Too thin. The muscle tone had slipped and her legs were disfigured by the multiple boat bites that have occurred. Unattractive and not pleasant to look at. As he lay there, partially awake, he started thinking about how this journey would end. The initial thrill and excitement of what he had done is losing its luster. His mind started racing ahead about how he would, someday, have to face up to the saying "all things end." *How will this end?* The thought had been entering is mind often lately. It gave him a sober and chilling feeling. It may come to something very bad. He eased out of the bed in the bow and headed for the stairs.

Chrystal had sensed that Chris was watching her and thinking about something. *Maybe me*, she thought. *No sex again this morning.* Which of course was just fine with her, but this had been occurring more often and causing her to feel that his physical interest in her was on the wane. There was one physical thing he could do, and maybe he was considering just that. She felt like a prisoner who was on death row and wondered when the executioner would approach her cell. She wasn't sure what he might have been thinking about. Probably nothing good, that's for sure. Her nerves were becoming frayed, and it was getting harder and harder to cope. She forced herself to get out of bed and prayed that somehow, someway, she would live through this nightmare.

Chrystal and Chris, now topside, were both under the tarp so that the sun was partially blocked. The shade was not much relief from the intense heat that was developing. She was the first to speak.

"The ocean looks like a frozen lake. It's so smooth. Undulation is hardly noticeable. I guess we are in for long hot days as we move south to whatever destination you have in mind." She was not sure what kind of mood he was in, so she busied herself arranging a few throw pillows while she waited for a response.

Chris looked very serious, and she even thought he might have looked worried about something. She wasn't sure, though. When he started to speak, it was like he was a teacher and not a twenty-two-year-old kidnapper.

"Chrystal, we have got to do something about our water supply." He went on to explain his deep concern. "When we left Hueneme, I estimated that we had close to 120 gallons of water. 100 gallons in the ship's water container and extra 20 gallons that I stocked aboard. We have been at sea for 35 days. So, I estimate that we have about 60 gallons left. We have not had a drop of rain, so we have not been able to capture any rainwater. We are about halfway to our destination." Chrystal's mind fixated on the words *we* and *destination*. It temporarily took her mind off the oppressive heat penetrating through the tarp. She wanted to interrupt him, but she did not. "We are using over the allocated amount that I suggested. We have to cut our water supply to two quarts a day. That's for both of us combined. I know that's about half of the four quarts of liquid a day that they say is necessary for humans to have, but we do not have that luxury. If we are dead in the water because of the doldrums, it could last for days. I can only use the motor for a very limited time to try and make any headway south. Like the water, our fuel is precious and conservation of gas is a must. No bathing, brushing teeth, bare minimum for food prep, toilet flush once a day. The potential danger for us could be immense if we do not prepare for the worst."

Both sat silently for what seemed like a long time before Chrystal broke the silence. "Okay, I absolutely will do whatever you say about saving water. Since you have never mentioned where we are headed, I wonder if you could fill me in on that." She didn't think he would reveal their putative destination, but it couldn't hurt to ask. To her absolute surprise, he told her where they were headed.

"Raraka Atoll, in French Polynesia. It's about another 1,800 miles south of the equator. I'll talk about that later. Right now, it's all about water and surviving. As a matter of fact, I recall a story my dad told me about how serious things can get when there is a severe lack of water. When the Spanish merchants and sailors were traveling these waters, one of the cargo items they had aboard were horses. They were going to introduce them to South America. After days of being trapped in the doldrums, their water was precariously low and the horses were depleting their water supply. They decided that the horses must be sacrificed and removed from the boats. They forced them off the boats into the sea. That's an example of how bad things can get. So Chrystal, let's brace ourselves for what lies ahead and survive. Water is our lifeline."

Chrystal watched Chris leave the helm to make some minor adjustments to the jib and mainsails so the *Columbia* could catch any zephyr that might pass by. It gave her a chance to digest the conversation that had just taken place as well as her perceptions in the bed this morning. Her brain was firing on all cylinders as she thought about how this morning had begun.

The lack of his routine and seemingly necessary sexual activity. This scared her because it showed a mood shift that might have deeper and more serious ramifications. His willingness to share "our destination." Not only was that an unexpected announcement, but it was loaded with a lot of unknowns. His lecture about water was sobering and suggested tough and scary times ahead. He topped it off with the horses being forced in the ocean because of the desperate water situation. She could just visualize the undernourished, dehydrated animals in a hopeless situation, floundering and thrashing in water, fighting for their lives as the boats sailed away. She shuddered with that image spinning around in her head. *That could be me.*

She had a lot on her mind as another boring day started to unfold. She looked east to watch the huge ball of sun popping up over the horizon welcoming her to another equatorial day. She was too flummoxed to pay any attention to the sun's good morning.

CHAPTER 19

The forty-one-foot *Columbia* was located approximately latitude 14° north and longitude 124° degrees, roughly one thousand miles west of the South American country of Columbia. Chris now believed that they were less than five hundred miles from the imaginary line designated as the equator. The air was hot, the water warm, and they were hardly moving. No longer did they see the swells created by the ocean's movement as they looked in any direction from the boat. There was no ocean spray as the bow sliced through small ripples, what were today's waves. Nor was there the noise of the salt-water bumping the boat with its unique sounds. The boat was steady, not rocking back and forth, or lifting up and down. No constant but gentle swaying as it reacted to the ocean's minimal movement. It was quiet. The hot blistering sun was starting to rise above the horizon. Chris and Chrystal would rather that another of nature's routines would give the sun a day off. Clouds. Both wondered if they were now about to experience what mariners have dreaded for years: the doldrums. They both thought so.

The effects of being at sea for so many weeks were becoming very notice-able in the appearance of the *Columbia's* two residents. What was not visu-ally apparent was the thought processes of both. The size of a sailboat is no problem when you go sailing for a few hours on a lake or at sea. It's fun. A change of pace. Something different. Size is not a concern. It's another matter when you have to coexist in a very limited space for extended time. Privacy is essentially nonexistent. So this morning they were just three or four feet apart, and neither one had much to say. Both ate breakfast and blankly stared at the sky and ocean. There would be no more coffee or tea. The menu did not change very much. Canned milk and cereal or a granola bar were the basic choices. Chrystal had made a mental note that if she survived this nightmare, she would never eat another granola bar. The main topic was generally the weather. Today was no exception.

"Chris, is this the first day of the start of the doldrums?"

"I don't think so. We are still two or three days north of the equator. I think it's just a passing calmness."

"Okay, I hope you're right. I guess I'm just getting nervous about what lies ahead." Never in her life had she said anything more on point.

"Chrystal, just because I have talked a lot about the equator and the doldrums, you should keep in mind it does not mean that we will have to endure harsh weather. It's just a possibility. We just have to be prepared to deal with it if we do."

The morning conversation ended, and both slipped into their daily routines, which meant minimal talking and maximum boredom.

Chrystal had nothing more to talk about to her abductor and left the helm and went down to the galley. Now alone, she mentally devoted her thought processes on how to survive and get away from the monster topside. The sad and depressing conclusion she always came to was that it seemed hopeless.

Live and escape. Live and escape. It was like breathing. In and out, in and out. That saying was her constant companion. She never stopped thinking of how, or if, it was possible to do so. After going through so many scenarios and ideas, she kept coming back to the fact that rescue was unrealistic. A thought that she repressed because she didn't think she could do it was to remove Chris from her life and the boat. It was a drastic thought, but drastic times require drastic measures. Her psychological make up was becoming more and more receptive to the idea she had to either incapacitate or kill him before he killed her.

The boat was barely moving in the calm sea and Chrystal's mind and body were slowly moving in rhythm with the motions of the boat. Succeed or fail, she decided that she was willing to risk everything in an effort to end her miserable and desperate situation. How to affect the demise of Chris would be her adopted challenge.

Reflecting back over the past weeks, she recalled that there were many times she could have killed him if she was inclined to do so. There were several knives in the kitchen, and it would be easy to stab him in his sleep. He was a very sound sleeper. One deep thrust to his heart with the large butcher knife should do it. Even if he didn't die immediately, she could hit him on the head with a heavy metal object or hold a pillow over his face until he stopped breathing. She shuddered as she thought about it, but she could just let him bleed out. Another possibility would be to watch for an opportunity to push him overboard. He was often very close to the rail with his back to her. It would be simple, with the element of surprise, to push him over the stainless steel safety lines that ringed the boat. Another thought occurred to her that helped her justify permanently killing Chris was, what was he thinking about or planning as far as her presence was concerned? Did he mention some island as a destination as a ruse just to give her false hope of survival? When she factored in all the possibilities for disposing of him, his demise was at the top of the list. Weeks ago, she dismissed the idea of going to that extreme because of the "then what?" factor. Now she was willing to accept being alone on the boat and trying to survive.

Because of the current wind, there wasn't any reason to be topside so she continued thinking about her newfound resolve to take some positive action. She had to come to grips with the notion that she might be able to actually kill another human being. She looked to the right of the stove and the knife rack that was below the two large stingrays she had made out of cork.

Snugly secured in the rack was the butcher knife. It was no longer a knife, it was a dagger waiting to be used in a homicide. No longer just a kitchen utensil. It was a weapon. She looked away. She remained seated and directed her attention to the general interior of the boat, and then, as if she had no control over her eyes, they returned to the knife rack. She got up, and after two steps, she removed the knife and felt the heft of the potential killing instrument. She felt a surge of power and strength as she squeezed the handle. It was sturdy and the blade was razor sharp. She noted that it was made in Germany, and she knew they made the best knives in the world. She replaced the knife in the rack. After she returned to the cushioned bench, she started counting on her fingers the reasons why she must follow through with the act. She stopped after counting to six:

1. Her intense hatred of Chris.
2. She no longer feared being alone on the sailboat.

3. She was confident that she could find the opportunity to rid herself of the monster one way or another.
4. She do not want die by his hand, or by circumstances over which she had little or no control.
5. She had flare guns. Maybe she'd get to use them.
6. Realistically, and of doubtful value, she could hoist the American flag upside down.

The meeting with herself ended. She felt relieved and rejuvenated and ready to face the days ahead. Her mind was made up. She got up from the bench and took another glance at the knife rack. As she contemplated the power the knife had just given her, a beam of sunlight flashed through the entrance to the galley. It caused the seven-inch blade to shine and glisten and beckon to her. She did not know if she was hallucinating or not, but she imagined and felt it was sending her a message. *I'll save you.*

As she was experiencing a newfound surge of hope, she noted that the wind was starting to pick up. The boat started reacting to the ocean's movement. It was a welcome sign. Her visual relationship with the knife ended when she heard Chris yell for her to come topside and help him with the sails. Before leaving, she had one last agenda item to consider. *When to act?* She decided that it would be after they passed the equator. Her reasoning was that if they hit the doldrums and then a severe storm developed, her chances of survival would lessen greatly.

Once topside and as she was untangling a sail, she asked Chris, "How much longer before we get to the equator?"

"If the wind picks up, like it seems to be doing, in two or three days." To herself, she thought, *Be prepared to die you bastard.*

CHAPTER 20

The precursor of the dreaded doldrums did not materialize and a change in the weather was developing. A northerly wind was increasing in strength, so Chris and Chrystal hoisted the sails. As the day lengthened, the wind continued to gain strength to the point that the spinnaker was now well in front of the bow and was in full bloom. As the bow sliced through the whitecaps and ocean troughs, the saltwater spray kissed everything topside. Chris was totally involved and enjoying every second of getting every ounce of speed possible out of the boat. It wasn't as if he had a time frame to be anywhere, it was just the challenge between the sea and him. He was engaged and enjoying himself. This was not the time to be thinking about the reality of his situation. In a way, though, he actually welcomed the respite from what had been occupying his mind the last several days. *What to do with Chrystal?* Actually, he knew he had a simple answer to that question.

The sun's work for the day was nearing its end. Its rays were starting to fade in the west, and dusk was slowly and inexorably absorbing the last shafts of daylight. Chris was sitting at the bow watching another day close. He was in a contemplative frame of mind. He had set the autopilot. The wind was holding steady, so there was no need to adjust the sails. The subject du jour for this evening was the same one that has been at the forefront lately. How is this experience going to end?

The staccato of the waves lapping the prow of the boat was rhythmic and pleasant to the mind and soul. As he listened to the ocean's symphony, he reflected on the situation he had caused and was now experiencing. What started out as an exciting and exhilarating plan for him to achieve was quickly losing its luster. All things end, and so must this trip. He felt extremely confident that he would never be caught for the disappearance of Chrystal. Therefore, he saw no reason to worry about police involvement. Considering that the only person he could talk to was his prisoner and forced lover, he felt isolated and alone. He found comfort talking to the sea. So, once again, he asked the ocean for advice. His question to his advisor, Neptune, the Roman god of the sea: "How should I end this mess I've created?" As he waited for an answer, he noticed a slight shift in the direction and the strength of the wind. He started the slow and short walk to the helm to trim the sails before adjusting the autopilot. Satisfied with the adjustments, he turned to go back to the bow. As he walked past the galley, and for no particular reason, he in looked to see what Chrystal was doing. What she was doing was indeed curious. Chrystal, who had her back to him, was holding a large knife in one hand, and with the other was cautiously and gently rubbing her finger across the blade as if she was testing its sharpness *What's that all about? Is she planning something?* Every vibration in his body suggested danger. He slowly continued the few remaining steps to the bow. Reflecting on what he had just observed, he finalized what the future held for the Malibu debutant. The god of the sea, Neptune, would get a new resident in his domain.

Now that he liked and adopted the idea about what to do with his passenger, he took a mental break from thinking about her day in and day out. He no longer would be constantly thinking about how this chapter in his life would end. His mind was made up. The current atmosphere, which was becoming more and more unenjoyable and now potentially dangerous, needed to end. Now he could hardly wait to get past the equator. He put the brakes on his thought processes about acting too quickly. He might need her to help manage and control the ship if a monstrous storm should happen. If she was needed or not, he'd find out in the next few days. *Be patient and just wait,* he reminded himself. He sighed and exhaled a couple of deep breaths and a sense of relaxation passed through his body. *Once she is gone, I'll be able to get some peace of mind.* He hoped he was right. He was not.

The sea can have an insidious and hypnotic effect on the psyche of a man. As he sat there staring blankly at the dark sea, his mind raced from one thought to another. No matter how hard he tried, three words kept reappearing in his mind, over and over again. He hated the fact that he could not stop the repetitiveness of them constantly appearing. *Kidnaper. Rapist. Murderer.* He shuddered as he sat there mumbling those words over and over.

"Gawd, that's me." As the night darkened, so did Chris's mood. The sea quit talking to him. He was on his own.

Hunched over, he just sat there staring at his deeply tan bare feet that were perched on a slightly raised rail that surrounded the edge of the cushioned seats in the helm. He was oblivious to everything around him. There was no Chrystal on the boat. No sea sounds or action. Just him and the boat. He gently rubbed and massaged his forehead with his fingertips as his mind drifted back to a time when he believed he was happy and life was not so complicated.

It was like he was no longer the evil and despicable human being that the three words he hated so much accused him of being. The words drifted away to the abyss of the inky dark world that surrounded his boat. He was with his mom and dad. His wonderful parents who loved him deeply. He was so happy then. His mind fixated on the mulberry tree that was so large that it seemed like it was trying to take over the entire property. It was like an umbrella that loomed over most of the house. He used to scamper up the tree, get firmly secure in its branches, and eat the ripe berries as he fantasized about a pretend world that was all his own. It was his escape world from reality—especially school, where he did not seem to fit in. His recall bounced from one aspect of his youth to another. The family dinners and the bonding with his parents at the dinner table; the birthday parties; and especially the family sailing trips and how his dad taught him how to be a superior and knowledgeable sailor. It was a sad recollection of the good times of the past colliding with his current reality. It was like the strong wind currents of the north smashing into the equally strong currents from the south at the equator. The results can be disastrous. His drifting to another time and place was interrupted when he noticed that the small, battery-operated bedroom light just below and slightly aft of where he was sitting was turned off. He decided it was time to bid adieu to the bow and make his way to the bed. As he walked down the steps to the galley, he made a mental note to check the knife rack as he passed by. He made a mental note to keep checking it.

CHAPTER 21

Hot, muggy, still, and not a drop of wind. The ocean was at a standstill. For the last three or four days, the sea slowly gave way to the fact that the wind was abating to the point that there wasn't the slightest detection of air movement. The air was so quiet that it was like being in a vacuum. Looking seaward, there was a sheen that glistened and covered the sea from horizon to horizon. It was like being in the middle of a desert and all there was is sand. Movement by sail was out of the question. The *Columbia* was dead in the water. With few tasks or things to do, the "crew" hunkered down in their favorite part of the boat, under the tarp that covered the helm. Less than six to eight feet apart, they sat and rarely spoke. Each reflected on their own private thoughts.

Chrystal's line of sight was westward, and she avoided looking at the rapist and kidnapper. Chris was sitting in a position that mimicked Rodin's sculpture The Thinker. His head was resting on his hand as he seemed to be staring downward in deep thought. He was! From time to time, he would lift his head and look hard and long at her. His question to himself was, *what happened to the most beautiful and sexy woman I risked so much for?* He studied her as she sat, slightly slouched over, staring westward.

In a mild state of confusion and wonder, he reflected back to the time when he used to spend hours studying the photos he had taken of Chrystal. He had her features memorized. She possessed absolutely every physical trait necessary to be called genuinely beautiful. He loved the photos of her face the best. He had enlarged several of them which allowed him to appreciate the depth and details of her features. Her face was more slender than oval. Her high cheek bones were extremely complimentary and were the highlight of her perfectly carved face, which enhanced her outstanding looks. Her lips were full, but not too full. Nestled behind her long and slightly curled eye lashes were eyes that sparkled and glistened like two precious sapphire gems. Her nose was perfect and proportionate. Her skin had the coloring of a young fawn. Her complexion was flawless. To him, her face was like a treasured painting, priceless and precious. Like all fine paintings, it should be framed. The frame should not detract from the painting itself but enhance its perfection. Her blond hair was the perfect frame.

Chris temporarily interrupted his recollection of Chrystal's face and remembered how many times he watched her as she walked to the spa, and on some occasions to Starbucks. It always excited him and aroused him. Her firm breasts that looked like they wanted to burst out of her form-fitted blouse. As he watched, her breasts had a suggestive and inviting movement to them when she walked. Oh, how he loved that! Her narrow waist accentuated the firmness and shape of her derrière that seemed to thrust forward with each step in a suggestive way. It was so sexy and a major turn on. In his imagination, he would visualize himself gently stroking and rubbing his hands up and down her fantastic legs as he explored every part of her body. These factors contributed to the genesis of his obsession that he must possess this living Venus de Milo.

His reminiscing was interrupted when out of his peripheral vision he saw a school of flying fish leaping and flying across the top of the water. Chris had always enjoyed the species and had done some research about their habitat and life. The fact that they were airborne suggested that they were trying to elude predators. They have the ability to swim upwards thirty miles per hour, propel out of the water, and glide the length of a couple of football fields. It was not uncommon that on occasion one would miscalculate and actually land on the deck of a sailboat. Chris heard it before he actually saw it. He looked in the direction of the sound and saw one flopping and slapping on the deck as it struggled to return to the sea. A sudden and impulsive urge developed.

Why don't I just do one good deed followed by a sinister deed? They can offset each other, right? The fish to safety and Chrystal to a watery grave. The thought and conversation with himself was an eyelash from happening. He felt himself start to rise from his seat and then he relaxed and eased back down. He stifled and controlled the urge to act. It was both stimulating and scary at the same time. Chris inhaled a deep breath of hot steamy air and got up from the bench that he was sitting on and walked over to the fish. With a quick swipe of his foot, he kicked it off the boat. Chrystal noticed this kind act without comment.

Just before the flying fish came aboard, Chrystal would occasionally glance over at Chris and briefly look at him as he sat there apparently deep in thought. She wondered what he was thinking about. Since they had been together for about six weeks in extremely close contact, they learn the nuances of one another. In this situation, Chrystal didn't like the feeling she was getting. She adjusted her line of sight away from looking directly at him to one that allowed her see him, yet give the impression she was looking away from him. The way he looked at her gave her the creeps. He had such a hard look on his face. Sinister, actually. *He's plotting, I can feel it*, she thought. Her perceptions and feelings were so strong it caused her to rethink what she could or would do to end this nightmare. She excused herself, not that formalities were necessary, and told Chris she'd be right back and walked below to the galley.

Now, out from under the tarp area and below deck, for some inexplicable reason, she started thinking about the swims that they took from time to time.

Occasionally on this sea voyage from hell, they would go for a swim. More often than not, nude. It served as a way to get some exercise as well as rinse and clean their clothes and bodies. It also served the purpose of cooling off. Sometimes they went together. Before entering the water, there was the mandatory scanning of the sea for sharks. If it looked safe, they would plan their entry. Chris would tie a strong, one-inch hemp rope around his waist and tie it securely to the boat. Chrystal could swim untethered and swim back to the rope to rest when she wished. They had done this many times when the conditions were right. It was relaxing and a good change of pace from the tedium and monotony that can develop at sea.

Sitting there in the galley, her mind was actively trying to come up with a way to address her intuitive feelings of gloom and despair when the idea of doing something during a swim started to gain momentum.

Before going back to the helm, she had another serious meeting with herself. Her observations and feelings were urging her to take control of the ship and eliminate Chris. *Eliminate, kill, use any word you wish, just get on with it.* She had convinced herself that she'd rather die trying to get free then have him kill her when he no longer needed or wanted her on the boat or in his life. Whoever took positive action first would be the survivor. Her mindset was that there might not be a tomorrow if she didn't take immediate action. There was little doubt in her mind that he would ultimately kill her. *I must act today but* how, was the major thought racing through her mind. She had not rejected the use of the butcher knife, but wanted a backup plan on how to eliminate the evil man who was ruining her life. Now all her mental facilities were fully charged. Her brain was in overdrive. As she looked around the area, her eyes stopped at the cork bulletin board and the grossly oversized stingrays she had made. Then it clicked. The Stanley boxcutter that she used to shape the cork projects.

With a smirk on her face, she headed topside to suggest they go for a swim.

CHAPTER 22

A very hot and tired looking Chris was sprawled out on the cushions under the tarp. He looked weary, fatigued, hot, and dehydrated. He paid no attention to Chrystal's approach as she sat down opposite him in the small amount of shade still available. As she looked at him, she thought the timing was perfect to see if he would go along with the idea of them cooling off by taking a refreshing dip in the sea.

"Chris, it seems warmer than usual and I'm so hot I'd really like to take a short swim to get some relief from this blasted heat. How about it? It would perk you up and make you feel better. I know it would make me feel better. What do you say?"

"I dunno. For some reason, I feel kinda beat. I doubt if I have enough energy to swim. I'm fairly comfortable just kicking back here in what little shade we have."

"You will just get more dehydrated laying there sweating. The ocean will cool you off. You'll feel better. Come on, let's do it."

"Well if you want to go that bad, I guess I'll give it a shot."

"Okay, great. I'll get the saltwater soap and a few items of your mom's clothes that are begging to be washed and meet you there."

A tinge of pure excitement and exhiliration was setting in as Chrystal went, ostensibly, to get the clothes and soap. Now alone and out of sight from Chris, she picked up a few items of Chris's mom's clothes that she had to wear every day. They had been left aboard. The clothes were for a much older person, but she was thankful to have them. The boxcutter was placed in the small bundle of clothes. It was all so surreal. If she failed in this mission to cause the death of a human being, she would be the one in the water watching the sailboat getting smaller and smaller, and farther and farther away from her. She steadied herself and was determined she had to go through with the act. "It's me or him," she whispered to herself. She was nervous and scared, but resolute, as she and her bundle of clothes ascended the stairs from the galley to commit the act and gain her freedom. It was time for Chris to remain in the sea, sans his boat.

As the usual procedure prior to entering the water was taking place, and Chrystal was studying the hemp rope very carefully. It looked thicker than she recalled when they went for swims previously. She felt certain the knife could slice the rope in half, but it might take a little more time than she thought. She made a mental note to make sure she allowed enough time to slice it in half. Chris yelled to her, "I'm all hooked up, let's go in."

"Okay, you go first," she responded.

With the lifeline rope securely attached to the boat and around his waist, Chris drifted away from the boat. Chrystal stalled for serval seconds and then slowly entered the water. She called out to Chris and yelled that she would quickly wash a couple of item and then join him. Now partially submerged in the water, she pretended that she was scrubbing one of the clothing items. She had one arm looped over the rope until it joined up with her other arm. From a distance of thirty feet or less, Chris could not see that she was actually removing the knife from the bundle of clothes. He was not paying any attention to her. With a small garment in her hand, which she hoped would shield what she was about do, she tugged on the submerged part of the rope to make it as taut as possible. She placed the blade of the knife on the rope and started pulling the blade back and forth in a sawing motion. It was harder to do than she thought. The rope was wet, and since it was underwater, harder to cut. She looked over at Chris and he was not aware of what she was doing.

As she was desperately sawing on the rope, Chris in a frantic, loud voice, screamed, "Get out of the water, sharks!" Chrystal looked up and saw several fins circling around and around. A panic mode immediately set in. Chris was swimming toward her as fast as he could yelling "Hurry! Hurry!" She was petrified. She dropped the knife but hung on to the clothes. By the time she climbed the three-step ladder that they used to get on and off the boat, Chris was right behind her scampering to get on deck. Once aboard, they both lay on their backs breathing hard reflecting on how close they came to being snatched up by a school of sharks and ripped apart and consumed.

Both were too numb to even talk. They just lay there thinking about what could have been.

Slowly, the day became like most of the days as the doldrums persisted. Chris was aft and Chrystal was at the bow. Each were internalizing their thoughts about whatever topic they wished to think about. Chris had two major things that preoccupied his thinking. Chrystal and the weather. Once the wind returned and he could hoist sails and be farther south of the equator, Chrystal had to be eliminated from his life. She had become a major liability and one he had to get rid of. He'd like to do it sooner, but the threat of a harsh and severe storm hitting them influenced him to wait. "I'll wait," he mouthed.

While Chris was mulling over his diabolic plans, Chrystal was doing something that she did all most every day: staring at the horizon. Today was different. She wasn't hoping to see a boat on the horizon that might mean rescue. Instead, she was going through a period of introspection. She was starting to have doubts if she really could take another person's life. As she reflected on what had just happened, she knew she had a chance to leave Chris to the sharks. Since cutting the rope was more difficult than she realized, she might not have time to untie the rope that was tied to Chris and tethered to the boat. She had thought about that earlier in her planning, but the knots (he had double knotted the ties) looked hard to untie. So she did not opt for that possibility. When she really had the chance to rid herself of him was when he was swimming back to the boat. She could have pulled the ladder back on to the boat and left him boat side without a way to get onboard. Once she was aboard, she reflected on why she didn't try to do that. Was it because she was so amped up that she wasn't capable of that option, or was it something deeper than that? She was tired of thinking about it, so she reverted back to her daily habit of scanning the horizon for anything different or out of the ordinary. She blinked her eyes several times to make sure of what she was seeing. There were several small clouds starting to take shape in the north. She looked south and the same thing was taking place. She sensed a weather change was pending.

Chris, a kidnapper and rapist, was first and foremost a good sailor. He, too, had seen the very distant clouds just barely visible on the far-off horizon.

Since they were now on the equator, he estimated that either a good wind or a storm was in their future. His inclination was a storm rather than a refreshing and welcomed wind. He started battening down the ship and asked Chrystal to help out. He told her that in all likelihood they could expect some rough times ahead. Chrystal was becoming apprehensive because of the uncertainty of the situation.

CHAPTER 23

A thin strip of ribbon, no longer than a foot and a half and an inch wide, was tied to the main mast. During the windless times for the past several days it was limp. It was depressing to look at when the best friend of a sailboat is the wind and it didn't move. It just hung down like the branches of a weeping willow tree. Snug against the mast and motionless. If a wisp of wind developed, it was so lightweight that it would easily pick up the slightest draft or whisper of wind.

"Chris, look up. Do you see what I think I see?" The ribbon wiggled. "Wind might be coming." He looked skyward up the main mast and agreed it was, in fact, moving.

"Let's hope it's just wind and not what could be our worst nightmare, a monster storm." The one thing they were both elated about was that they would be moving and not just sitting there motionless.

Much of the day was spent checking and rechecking the boat to make sure it was prepared for whatever was in store for them in the coming days or hours ahead. As Chris studied the specks of clouds forming on the north and south horizons, his instincts were to get ready for whatever Mother Nature might have in store for them. Even though there were no assurances whatsoever of harsh weather incoming, the real possibility that it might happen caused an element of electricity and excitement to develop. As far as Chrystal was concerned, there was also an element of fear. Prior to being a forced passenger on her floating prison, she had spent very little time at sea. She wondered if she had the physical and mental constitution to deal with massive turbulence of the ocean over an extended period of time. She was about to find out.

Once the sun set and darkness changed day to night, each of them had developed certain habits during the evening hours. Since their backgrounds were so very different, things to talk about were limited. This, of course, factored in with Chrystal's hatred of Chris and also inhibited her desire to talk at all. Typically, Chris would tinker with the engine or get engrossed with charts and navigational equipment. It seemed that everything that interested him was about boats. There was limited reading material aboard for Chrystal. The few magazines aboard had to do with the care of plants and flowers. There were a few whodunit books by well-known writers who were so prolific that they always seemed to have a new book out. They were not helpful. Tonight was just like many of the others. Boredom reigned.

There was one thing that was constant each and every night, and it was that Chrystal hated the time that they went to bed. She never knew if it would be another night of forced sex or she could hug her side of the small bed and be left alone. During the past few nights, she was thankful that his libido allowed her avoid enduring the pain and anguish of his unwanted and detested passion. Maybe more important than that was it lessened the possibility of her getting pregnant, which was a dread that had haunted her throughout the acts that had taken place over the past weeks. To date, she had escaped that very unwanted possibility. She was absolutely certain that Chris could care less if a pregnancy happened. She was disposable and therefore the fetus would meet the same fate she would. Death.

Chrystal was the first to go bed. It wasn't long after she lay on her side of the bed waiting to see what was on the bedroom agenda tonight that Chris came to bed. Lately, he had not been so, what he would term, "romantically attracted" to her. She understood why. How could she possibly have the charm and beauty that caused him to abduct her? When she looked at herself in the mirror, she reminded herself of pictures she saw when looking at prisoners of war who survived the Bataan Death March during World War II. "What can you expect," she said to the mirror. Food was scarce and what limited food they ate was not very nourishing. There was barely enough water to drink. Her ribcage had lost so much skin that her bones were visible. Her high cheekbones that highlighted her beautiful face now seemed to protrude outward and distort her facial features. It caused her face to look gaunt. Her hair that was once so beautiful was now stringy, matted, and dirty. The wind and sun had destroyed her skin. It was blistered, peeling, and blotchy. After all the self-evaluation of her appearance, she waited to see what would take place in the bow of the boat tonight.

The boat was gently rocking side to side. The movement was slightly more noticeable than last night. Chrystal waited. "Chrystal, I noticed something that is concerning and I want to talk to you about it."

"Oh, what's that?"

"The rope that was tied to me when we went swimming"

"What about it?" Chrystal wondered if he'd noticed the slicing of the rope and anticipated that he'd ask about it.

"It looked like it had been partially cut with a knife. Did you try to cut it?"

"Of course not. I was in the water with you. Did you see me cutting or trying to slash that thick rope? Did you see me with a knife? You were right behind me when we got aboard the boat, and we laid down on the deck on the deck side by side. I never had a knife. Did you check to see if all the knives are in the knife rack? My answer is I have no idea what you are talking about and why you are asking me all these questions."

"Okay, maybe it snagged or got caught on something and I just hadn't noticed it before. Forget about it." His inclination was that she was lying, but he did not see her do anything to the rope and all the knives were on the rack. It really didn't matter. *She'll be in the water soon enough without any rope attached.*

"Oh, Chrystal, one last thing. I think that starting tomorrow we better start doing watches at night. We'll talk about it in the morning."

Chrystal waited. She was relieved when she perceived that he was going to leave her alone and go to sleep.

Just before she drifted off, she noticed that the boat was rocking noticeably more than a few hours ago. Although she enjoyed the movement, she wondered if it was the precursor of a weather change. That was the last thought she had before she fell asleep.

CHAPTER 24

The mainsail was up about the same time as the sun. Chris and Chrystal were both standing on the bow enjoying the warm, almost hot breeze that was now quite noticeable as they sailed south. After so many days without wind, it was a welcomed change. If there was a category for the least likely conundrum, it was now standing on the deck of the boat. Both outwardly enjoying the early morning making its daily appearance. Almost in unison, they inhaled the aromas around them as the day started to unfold. The gentle but steady breeze kissing their faces as they faced into the wind. Both looking comfortable and enthusiastic as if they were enjoying a pleasant day sailing. What one could not know is what they were thinking about how and when one might eliminate the other. If they would openly share what they were thinking, they would both agree that there would be one less crewmember aboard, and soon.

Chris stared at the small ridge of darkening clouds in the far-off distance that seemed so far away that it would take a very long time to reach them, if they ever did. He knew that was wishful thinking. His assessment was that in a day or two, severe weather would hit and they had better be ready to deal with it. He left the bow and asked Chrystal to come with him because there was a lot of precautionary tasks that needed to be done. The tone of his voice and the urgency of the request was somewhat unnerving, yet exciting as well. She followed him to the cockpit.

It was time to batten down the boat. They started in the galley. Anything that might become a flying missile as the boat was tossed and bounced about during a turbulent and churning sea needed to be secured. Flying objects could be dangerous to them as well as the boat. They checked to make sure that the portholes were tightly closed. A swamped boat could become a sunk boat. As an added safety measure, a bucket was wired to the galley table, which was bolted to the floor, to be used in case they had to bail water. While Chrystal thoroughly secured items in the galley, Chris did the same thing in the engine compartment. Both kept quite busy for several hours before they took a short break under the tarp covering the cockpit. This reminded Chris that he would need to remove the tarp sometime during the course of the day. After a short break, the next thing on the safety agenda was to instruct Chrystal on the use of safety lines and the sea anchor.

There was no intention of having a doomsday type of atmosphere when teaching Chrystal about the importance of safety lines and why and how to use a sea anchor, but it certainly was in his best interest that she knew when and how to use them. He gave her a demonstration on both subjects. She was an attentive listener and only needed Chris to go over the subjects one time. He explained that the tethered safety lines were to be clipped onto a clasp that is attached to her vest. On the other end of the line, it is attached to a similar setup on either side of the cabin or cockpit. He emphasized to her that the lines cannot be too long because if they are, they could be tossed overboard and hung up on the side of the boat, still attached, and drown. During his educational presentation about safety lines, he told her that lines six to eight feet were ideal under most circumstances. Together they practiced hooking up the safety lines several times. He made her go through the drill over and over. She felt like it was like a fire drill in school. Year after year, she did the drills, but there was never a fire. Another thought that passed through her mind, as diabolical as it was, that one might be able somehow ensure that the line was disconnected. Something to think about.

She paid little attention to his explanation of the use of sea anchors as he went into great detail about the function they serve. Her feelings were that if the boat was going to be at the control of the sea, so be it. Ride out the storm and go from there. She could care less that a sack-like item tied to the bow, on a fairly long line, helped keep it into the wind while a similar arrangement was dropped into the sea at the stern to help keep the boat straight and avoid drifting too much. When the class on anchors and safety lines was over, they both phased back to their usual routines. The one thing they both did was not talk to each other very often. They seemed so preoccupied with something and that "something" was getting through this storm and end up on the boat, alone.

The one exception to this being another long, uneventful day, was the very light but constant wind that allowed the mainsail to do its job of moving the boat southward. Another exception was the small, dark clouds they noticed earlier in the day that seemed a little bit larger, but still quite far away.

Daylight started to show signs of giving way to dusk. It was like the changing of the guard. One weather scenario giving way to another. As the sky inevitably darkened, the nightly diamonds started to become more and more brilliant, and without fail, Venus settled into its nightly position snuggled up next to the moon. Eternal companions. Despite all the negativity swirling around the abductor and abductee, they both were, at least at the moment, enjoying the serenity of a beautiful evening. Chrystal, without saying anything, went below for the rest of the night. Unbeknownst and unfortunately for her, Chris was contemplating his last sexual act with her on the eve of the forthcoming storm and her last forty-eight hours alive.

Despite her diminishing looks and her fading appeal, Chris was coming to grips with the fact that any future sexual activity with other women was uncertain. He realized and accepted the fact that the current saga would end, and soon, so why not take one last bite out of the apple. With that mindset, he descended the steps to the bed in the bow.

Chrystal, over the last several weeks, had learned to pick up on Chris's nuances when it came to his bedtime behavior. No matter what he might do, she despised being so close to him in the small bed they had to share. There was no avoiding touching each other throughout the night. So the reality was that she was trapped and lying next to her was an over-sexed, muscular, testosterone-driven, and potentially aggressive young man. She was thankful that for the last few nights he had left her alone. Tonight, she gauged his mannerisms as he approached and removed what little clothing he had on and lay next to her. It was obvious that tonight he would have his way with her. So the torturing, disgusting, and unpleasant nightmare began.

Chrystal turned her small pillow over so she could bury her head on the dry side. The other side of pillow was wet, not from the exertion that developed during the rape, but from her tears and sobbing as she lay there physically and mentally spent, reflecting on how she was just treated and used. As she lay there unable to sleep, she resolved that she would no longer submit to being sexually and physically abused. She would have taken that stance much sooner, but she was constantly trying to figure out how to intelligently manipulate what was taking place and end this madding situation. She did have a plan of escape, but a series of circumstances needed to be in place in order for it work. Consequently, she never had taken a life-or-death stance with Chris. Since the "circumstances" had yet to develop, and they might not, she decided that she could no longer live with herself if she did not defy him. If death is what might occur, she vowed to accept it over her current situation, which to her was a living death. Content that her resolve was firm, she was now mentally prepared to accept whatever lay ahead.

Before fatigue and exhaustion gave way to sleep, she thought she heard a distant rumbling noise. It sounded so far away. She wondered if it was thunder. She fell asleep thinking the sound was the precursor of the storm they had been anticipating for the past several days.

CHAPTER 25

The rocking of the boat had noticeably changed. The passengers were aware that they might have to hold on to something, or else they could possibly stumble. So both of them were cognizant of the need to be more cautious as they went topside to check out the weather. The small darkening clouds that yesterday seemed so far away were much closer and darker. There was less blue in the sky. It seemed like the sun was trying to make its daily appearance, but the cloud banks were interfering with that effort. It was not raining, but there was a sensation of moisture in the air. The heretofore flat and calm sea now had a choppiness that accounted for the increase of the boat's rocking. Chris and Chrystal did not speak as they individually assessed the changing weather pattern. The developing storm gave Chris a feeling of excitement. Chrystal was getting nervous and worried. She had no idea what to expect and it was unsettling. If she didn't hate Chris so deeply, she would have welcomed a hug.

The storm was inevitable. The difficult part was waiting. Both of them tried to keep busy as they went about doing various chores on the boat as they constantly checked out the sky and sea. The day actually seemed longer than prior days. There was that feeling of being tired of waiting out what might happen, yet wanting it to take place, and soon. Get it over with. But wait they must. The weather with all its complexities would develop as it had for ages on its own timetable. When all the components are in alignment, its force and power would be unleashed. So the day slowly unfolded with the morning hours slowly giving way to the afternoon hours as the storm countdown continued.

As the chop and swells of the ocean continued to increase, Chris thought it was timely to mention an additional chore for Chrystal, as well as offer her some advice. He wanted her to devise any system she could create to catch water once the rain started and before the wind got too strong. He correctly calculated that once the storm ended, they would soon run out of water to drink if their supply wasn't increased. As he was expressing that thought to Chrystal, she locked on to the word "they." He also told her that after the storm ended, they would only be a day or two from ostensibly where they could get food, water, and fuel. That word again, "they." She still did not trust him and her life continued to be in immediate danger, yet he frequently included her when he spoke of the future. *Perhaps he is just trying to falsely assure me that my safety is nothing to be worried about. He is dead wrong if that's what he thinks*, she reminded herself. For the moment, she put personal concerns aside and started thinking about the collection and storage of water. "I'll figure out what I can do about the water right away. Oh, what's the advice you have for me?" she asked.

"I'll get back to you in a sec. I want to double-check the rigging and the boom while I have a chance. I think they are okay, but I want to make sure."

As Chrystal was arranging various ingenious ways to catch rainwater and have it flow into the five-gallon water bottles that were mostly empty, Chris returned. He told her that he wanted to talk to her about the intake of food and liquids since he knew that the boat would mostly be at the mercy of the sea. It could be an unimaginable physical and mental experience for an extended period of time. They both knew that they were low on almost everything, but they still had some water and a few canned goods. He suggested that she drink as little as possible and not eat much. Another suggestion was to try to get by with some toast and applesauce for the next few hours. Something easy to digest. He could tell that Chrystal was starting to get scared the more he talked about his concerns about their well-being and safety. He tried to comfort her by telling her of his experiences. In the long scheme of things, the storms were generally over rather quickly. "We will make it." he assured her. She was indeed getting a little apprehensive about the forthcoming storm, but she also wondered about some of the words he had been using in their conversations. *We. They.* What was he planning or thinking about? She would give that question a lot of thought.

Dusk was approaching and so were their new companions, the ominous dark clouds. The chop in the sea was increasing and the boat was reacting accordingly. Before it got too dark, Chris decided to set up the sea anchor.

It was his speculation that by morning the storm would no longer be just a possibility, but a reality. He was hopeful that he would be able to avoid too much drift and keep the boat into the wind, so both of them, working as a team, went about setting up the sea anchor apparatus. Chris was annoyed with himself for not getting the anchor in place sooner. The movement of the boat made it necessary for them to put on their vests and hook up their safety lines. She was glad she was tethered and reasonably safe and actually somewhat impressed with how she performed as a neophyte sailor.

Chris was satisfied that the sea anchor was now in place and working properly. Still tethered, they both stood in the cockpit and watched the storm develop. The ocean and sky seemed to have melded together so they were completely surrounded by blackness. They had no point of reference. No moon, no stars. The compass was the only assuring feature they had that they were in fact moving in a southerly direction.

Chis preceded Chrystal in detaching his safety line and went below. Chrystal was right behind him and stayed within arm's reach. The boat was gyrating with just enough force that it was necessary to pay careful attention to each movement. Chrystal carefully reached the first step then stopped and looked skyward. A raindrop gently landed on her cheek before falling to the deck. It was nature's notification that the storm had arrived.

Once belowdecks, they quickly decided that the turbulence was very strong and would only increase. The worst place to try and sleep was in the bow of the boat. The best place in rough sea is in the middle of the boat. The galley floor. Chris moved the mattress to the center of the boat and used bungie cords to secure it in place. He also laid some clip-on straps near the bed that could be strapped over their bodies as they lay on the floor. If the rocking and tossing became too violent, this precaution could save them from being seriously injured. Chris's dad used this procedure on two different occasions in previous storms to help him when they were caught in some very heavy sea. It helped, but he still was sick as a dog. Watching all the prep work taking place was so nerve-racking that Chrystal was starting to think she might have a panic attack. The odds were mounting that such an attack was just around the corner.

CHAPTER 26

Chrystal and Chris were below deck in a holding pattern waiting for whatever fury nature wrought. The behavior of the boat's reaction to the sea was such that they could still move about, but cautiously. They were being jostled about just enough that sleep would be very difficult. Chrystal, for the first time, started noticing signs of seasickness. Hour after hour of extreme and vigorous movement is an experience that even seasoned sailors often have a hard time adjusting to without being adversely affected. Chrystal was looking pale and ashen. What was so upsetting and depressing was what was now taking place was just the beginning of the storm, and these feelings and sensations might go on for days. She was starting to have doubts if she could physically and mentally cope with what loomed ahead. She had to constantly remind herself that there wasn't anything she could do but try to endure and survive. It did not help her mental processes as she noted that Chris looked perfectly comfortable even though the boat was rocking and swaying more vigorously than it had the past several weeks.

Hardly speaking to each other, they hunkered down holding on to something firm enough to prevent falling to the deck or ricocheting off the sides of the galley walls. Time seemed to stand still. There was nothing to do but think and wait. Chrystal also had to fight off getting ill.

It seemed like it should be morning and that some daylight should be happening even though only a few hours had elapsed. The battery of the only clock aboard had stopped working a few days ago, and they had to rely on nature to give them any idea of time. Sitting there and waiting, killing time, they were serenaded by boat sounds. Rigging that jingled and clanked monotonously. Earlier during the southern sail, the sound was an expected part of the genre of sailing. Now with stronger winds, the sound was faster and louder. What was once a pleasant and melodic sound was now becoming irritating and annoying. The "Rig Rhapsody," unaware of its negative effect on the boat occupants, would play on until the wind decided otherwise.

The constant slapping of the rigging had competition when it came to sounds that never seemed to stop. Second after second, minute after minute, hour after hour, the slapping and smacking of the sea against the boat was one of the competitors. Sometimes the choppy sea hit with such force that she wondered if the boat would shatter. For Chrystal, it was nerve-racking and scary. She knew that the storm was just warming up and the worst was yet to come. The disgusting aspect of the situation was made worse by the fact that at this moment in time there was nothing she could do about it. As she reflected about all the things that had happened to her since her imprisonment and forced captivity, she was starting to worry if she'd live through this nightmare and survive. At this despondent moment she looked over at Chris and he was sitting in a chair that was bolted to the deck and was actually asleep. She wanted to get the butcher knife and thrust it into his heart. "Then what would I do? Not now," she counseled herself. As she sat there recalling all she had gone through, seeing him asleep actually rejuvenated her will to fight and survive. Never give up. That was her mantra, and she would follow it even if it cost her her life.

The night dragged on. The boring and tedious night, like all nights, had yet to give way to the morning. It was Chris's intuition that daybreak was about to happen. He looked out of the starboard porthole but was unable to discern if he could see any signs of daylight. He slowly opened the galley door, just enough to look about. He saw a small fissure of light between the huge and very dark clouds that seemed to have the boat surrounded. The wind was strong and loud as it cascaded over the helm carrying missiles of saltwater that smacked him in the face.

"It's nasty out there, but I think it's still safe to check out the boat. If you want to join me, put on some foul-weather gear and your vest and hitch up your safety line." After one of the longest nights of her life incarcerated in the galley, she could hardly wait to yell back that she'd join him, which she did.

Very carefully, they inched their way topside hanging onto anything that was solid and strong enough to let them move safely. The mixture of rain and wind definitely influenced how they could move about. They were hunched over and steadying themselves and about to take their first steps when lightning bolts exploded across the entire northern horizon. Brilliant, silver streaks of electricity took over the sky. The electrical bolts were raining down in vertical and horizontal patterns. They watched the ultimate fireworks display with a sense of excitement as well as fright, which pulsated through their bodies. It was truly a magnificent sight, but scary, too. They were about to see explosion after explosion of bolts falling down out of the heavens time after time. Enthralled at what they were watching, they almost forgot about the thunder that surely would follow. Light travels faster than sound, so it took a few seconds before the first clap of thunder reached the boat. It was so loud and thunderous, Chrystal thought it would crack the sea and earth in half. She thought that if the world should ever come to an end, it would be with sounds like those she was feeling at that moment.

Chrystal was so awestruck by what she was watching that she really hadn't paid that much attention to the sea's behavior. It was getting lighter now, so she had a chance to check it out. The one thing that she noted that differed from yesterday was that the ocean was developing troughs that made the boat slide down one side of the trough and then up the other side. She speculated that the dips up and down was around three to four feet. She hoped they would not get any bigger. As the boat swayed back and forth, up and down, with an occasional lurch, it instinctively caused her to tighten her grip on her safety line. She steadied herself as she carefully made her way to the cockpit.

During her inspection of the area, she did note that the small crack over the glass compass had not gotten any bigger, so she was glad about that. Her feedback to Chris would be on the positive side as far as any damage to the helm. It was difficult retracing her steps back to the galley entrance. Each step she took was carefully thought out before the next one. The boat was under considerable stress as the ocean and wind mercilessly hammered away. The motion never stopped and started to get worse. The wind seemed out of control and punished everything in its path. This small boat was its victim. She was almost at the first step when the boat dipped into a trough at least ten to twelve feet deep. When the bow reached the bottom of the steep drop, the boat started the climb up the other side of the wave. The angle of the upward thrust caused the bow of the boat to point skyward.

Chrystal braced herself with all her strength to a bar railing as she anticipated the next jolt. Hoping that she could hang on long enough to take the last step to the galley. She was petrified that if she didn't make that step, the impact of the boat crashing at the bottom of the nest trough would cause her to lose her grip and be tossed about topside like a rag doll, or tossed overboard still attached to her safety line. She was struggling to hang on to the bar. Her hand started to loosen and slip off the bar. Even in this life-and-death situation, she now knew why Chris told her to check the helm. She wouldn't make it back alive. He would unlatch the safety line and let her fall into sea. Just as her hand was slipping off the bar, Chris reached for her. He grabbed the hood of her wet weather jacket and it slipped off her head. He then, luckily, managed to snatch her by her hair and pull her to the top of the stairs. He literally dragged her down the stairs where the two of them lay exhausted and breathless. Both were thinking their individual thoughts.

Why did I save her? I have to eventually get rid of her.

Maybe, after all, he will not murder me.

Chris had been watching the situation as Chrystal struggled to return from the helm, but the unexpected seriousness of what was taking place made it so dangerous that he was afraid that if he intervened too soon they both would be doomed. The combination of Chrystal's grit and determination and his timing of the rescue allowed her to live another day. Possibly one of the few remaining days she had left.

CHAPTER 27

Hour after hour, the roar of thunder created an atmosphere that was like watching a movie with eerie background music that let the viewer knew something strange or bad was surely about to happen. Adding in the wind and rain pelting the boat and the sky that was aflame with the lightning bolts zigzagging across the sky, the scene was set for something negative and unwelcome to take place.

After the harrowing experience that just happened, Chris told Chrystal that she was not to go topside unless he approved. She nodded that she understood. Especially after what had just taken place. After the rescue, she reflected on how she could have been seriously injured or possibly killed. She was visibly shaken. Her nerves were shot. She had no desire to engage in talking. She was becoming dehydrated and very seasick. There was absolutely no way to escape from the relentless and constant beating the boat was absorbing as the ocean tossed it around like a cork bobbing up and down in turbulent water. To try and ensure safety and allow for some sleep, Chis, who was not feeling too well himself, managed to strap her to the cabin floor with straps, rope, and cord. It is the most stable area of the boat. This would prevent her from being injured as the severe rocking of the boat took place hour after hour. She could hardly move anyway because of her weakened condition. As she lay there, she thought death would be a welcome relief. Only a few hours had elapsed, but it seemed like she had been lying there for at least a day. She was so sick. Unable to eat or drink, and the urge to regurgitate was her constant companion. She was miserable. She wished she would pass out so that she'd be unaware of what her body and her state of mind were going through.

There was no respite from the storm throughout the long—very long—night. Chrystal seemed to phase in and out of consciousness. During one instance of awareness, she thought about a laundromat. Instead of clothes being in the dryer, it was her bouncing and flopping about. Another image was during the wash phase. The spin cycle was spinning and twirling her around and around. The timing for such imagery couldn't have been worse. The nausea and suffering stayed with her hour after hour. The only relief was when she would slip into a coma-like state. There was little either of them could do. The remedy was simply to ride out the storm. That was the diagnosis and solution.

The storm continued unabated for the next day and night. There was little change in the severity of the storm. There was one notable change, though. Chris had managed to get Chrystal to sip some water and nibble on some stale crackers. It was like spoon feeding a baby. Just a little bit at a time. Miraculously, that seemed to help. Ever so slowly, her system, both physically and mentally, started to improve. As Chrystal's ability to adjust to the perpetual and constant movement of the boat improved, she started to reflect on how she was saved from certain and serious danger by Chris. The question that was indelibly fixated in her mind was *why?*

Chrystal decided that she'd ease into a conversation with Chris about why he rescued her from being seriously harmed or killed. Since it was still too dangerous to leave the galley and there was so much downtime, she thought she'd take a stab at trying to figure out what he had in mind once the storm stopped. Chris, who was standing with his legs well apart, was leaning against a table that was anchored to the floor. His sea legs served him well. He rocked and pivoted with the boat as it swayed and lurched. He looked to be in a reflective mood. He had not spoken for some time and was standing a few feet from her. She had no idea what he was thinking about, if anything.

Repressing all her feelings about how this human being had harmed and hurt her for weeks and caused her to exist in an atmosphere of uncertainty, she nevertheless decided to try and be pleasant as she pressed on with an idea to ask some questions. With an angelic tone in her voice, she asked him, "Chris, the storm will end soon and I would like to know what is in store for me. What are you planning? It's driving me crazy not knowing. Will you share what you have in mind? Please, please, I beg you to tell me."

Chris was caught off guard by the unexpected question and her sincerity. He looked hard at her. The look he had in his eyes was the same as when he aggressively and brutally raped her for the first time. He continued to stare at her without speaking. He started rubbing his hand over his unshaven face over and over again. He was thinking about how to respond or if he would. His response was not reassuring.

"I'm not sure what I'll do. I'm still thinking about it. You'll find out when it's time. That's all I have to say. Think about something else. You'll find out about what I am going to do when I feel like telling you. That's it."

It was a chilling response and the tone in his voice said that the conversation was over. He turned his back to her and continued to lean against the table looking blankly at the starboard porthole. The only sounds were the creaking and laboring of the boat as it fought back the efforts of the storm that was trying to destroy it.

Chrystal was flummoxed as she thought about what had just occurred. Her inner voice was now very active. *He nursed me back from the depths of my seasickness. How can he switch from a helpful person to such a scary and unpredictable man?* It was so hard to figure out that it was disturbing. *Just now, he was harsh and cold in the way he spoke to me. He had never slapped or hit me during this maddening trip, but for just an instant, I thought he might.* Silence was now the norm in the galley. Boat sounds were the only noises to be heard. She continued to be confused, worried, and scared as she looked at Chris's back. He had turned away from her. Those very feelings were exacerbated when she recalled how certain he was that he would never be caught. *He'll do something to me, I'm sure,* she thought. *And soon.*

Chris quit staring out the porthole and sat on one side of the galley table. His head was bent over as he rested it on his folded arms. He did not look at Chrystal. The atmosphere suggested that he did not have any intention of talking to her and wanted to be left alone. Alone with his thoughts, he just wanted the night to end and see what the weather had in store for them tomorrow. His intuition said that the storm, ever so slightly, was starting to ease, but going topside was still a dangerous outing. He was actually fairly comfortable in the position he chose. So much so that he fell asleep.

Chrystal was sitting across the table from Chris, less than four feet from him. She could tell he was falling asleep. Within arm's reach was the knife rack and the eight-inch butcher knife. Its sturdy glistening blade beckoned to her. *Use me. End this madness. Do it now. It's your last chance.* It was like she was being hypnotized. It kept talking to her, and it was consuming her. She was seething with so much anger and hate that she wanted to thrust the blade deep into his back and let him suffer like she had. She was slowly building up enough nerve to act and follow the power of the knife. As she started to reach for it, an unusual and concerning sound topside occurred that instantly woke Chris. Like most seasoned sailors, at any sound of occurrences that are not routine, there is an instant reaction. He bolted upright from his slumped sleeping position and started listening intently. It sounded like metal banging against the boat in the cockpit. It was not hitting in just one place. The clanking of whatever it was struck the boat in several different places, but all in the cockpit.

"Something's loose," he announced, and told Chrystal that he must check it out.

As he was putting on his rain slicker and vest that would be hooked to his safety line, he kept looking at Chrystal. He sensed something peculiar about her demeanor. She had a guilty look. *Why?* he wondered. He dismissed thinking about her for the moment. He had to check out what was going on in the cockpit. Before he left the galley, he reminded Chrystal that the storm may be easing some, but it was still dangerous topside, so as a precautionary measure, he asked her to hook up and be at the ready if something untoward should occur.

She yelled okay just as he opened the door. He could not hear her. The power of the wind was so strong and loud that he mouthed, "What?" She held her hand up with a thumbs up signal. He nodded his head and mouthed, "Okay." Carefully, he stepped out into the storm. The irony of the last few minutes was not lost on her. Five minutes, ago she was going to kill him, and now she was his lifeline.

CHAPTER 28

Before taking his first step, Chris studied the weather conditions. He was temporarily blinded by the sheets of rain that were whipping across the boat nearly horizontally. He partially opened his eyes, but just enough so he had some vision. The force of the rain peppered his face with such force that it felt like shards of glass hitting him. He steadied himself by gripping a hand bar as he looked at the action of the sea. The wind whipped across the water with such power that the number of white caps gave the ocean an appearance of white foam. The depth of the troughs seemed to be smaller. Maybe six feet or less, but deep enough to make the boat very unstable for walking. He duly noted the deck awash with seawater skimming across the route he would have to walk to the cockpit. The only positive thing he observed was a thin line of light on the horizon. Dawn was trying to make its appearance where there were fewer clouds. The one last thing he did to ensure his safety before trying to figure out what was causing the noise he heard from the galley was to check the length of the lifeline he would use. He had two lengths: a six-foot line and a thirteen-foot line. Since he didn't know exactly what area he'd have to check, he opted for the longer line. The six foot length was considered the safer of the two because there is less chance of being flipped overboard. As the boat rocked, rolled, and dipped, cautiously and slowly, he started to make his way to the cockpit. Standing by and at the ready, if needed, Chrystal watched Chris safely traverse the eight to ten feet to the helm. So far, so good.

Chris heard a crackling sound and then felt something crunching beneath his feet. He looked down and whatever it was under his deck shoes, and it was shiny and glistening. Looking closer, he could see that there were a few pieces of glass strewn across the deck. He immediately looked at the compass. Most of the glass covering it was gone. The wind and rain had broken the glass and damaged the directional needles as well other component parts of the compass to the point that it was now useless. He had no time to waste on this bad luck. He had to figure out what caused the breakage and prevent it from causing any further damage.

Chris held on to a hand bar that was attached to the cabinets where he now stood at the helm. He had his legs spread fairly far apart for balance as he waited to see or hear what was damaging the boat. The sea was relentless as it tossed the boat about in the ocean just like a kayak as it twisted, spun, and made its way through the extremely turbulent water while running the rapids. Water was cascading across the deck giving him pause and concern about leaving the helm to examine the boat. He considered retuning to the galley, but quickly dismissed that thought. He had only been out of the galley and at the helm for less than a couple minutes when he heard what sounded like a piece of metal striking very close to where he was standing. As he looked in the direction of the sound, he saw a rope dangling from the boom that was swaying back and forth in the violent wind. Still attached to the rope was a metal block the size of a grapefruit, which was part of a pulley system that is used to secure the boom when it's not in use.

The rope had become partially detached from the boom and was swinging back and forth at the whim of the wind. It was just long enough to reach the instrument panel in front of the helm, which caused the damage to the compass. Chris quickly and correctly assessed that he had to harness in the flying missile before it did any more damage. Under normal sailing conditions, it would have been easy to do, but not this morning. He decided that he would inch his way alongside the boom until he reached the pulley system and then slowly reel in the rope and tie it off. It was a difficult task. He had to maintain his balance. He never took his eyes off the rope and tethered block as he approached it. It was a slow and tedious job, but his patience and determination paid off. He was able to reach the rope, secure the line, and remove the metal block. Satisfied that it was safe to return to the galley, he started what he knew was the most dangerous time topside. The sea troughs had been fairly predictable, averaging less than five feet. At that depth, it was extremely dangerous for anyone to be topside for any reason. The bow of the boat would rise up the side of the trough and then, at the crest, slide down the other side and smack the bottom with such force that the boat strained to not break up, fall apart, and be consumed by the violent storm. The timing of each step was critical. He had to posture himself in such a way that he could sway and rotate with the motion of the boat. He was now ready to take his first step. When the boat was at the bottom of the trough, he would cautiously take a step, possibly two, if he had time.

Crouched and shielding herself the best she could from the wind and relentless rain, Chrystal watched Chris as he prepared to return to the galley. It was a frightening drama to witness. As she waited and watched what was unfolding, she realized the importance of his survival if she was to live through this ordeal. She had on her rain gear and her safety line was attached. As directed, she was at the ready to help out in any way she could.

As Chris took a step toward the bow, it shot skyward as it tried to climb the face of the wave. It was huge. The angle of the boat was so severe that it looked like it might not make it and either pitchpole or capsize. Chrystal felt like her head was going to detach itself from her shoulders. She gripped the hand bar with both hands as hard as she could. If the boat did not flip over, she knew what was ahead. It was like a roller coaster ride. The chair had climbed to the top of the ride and was now ready to take the severe and sharp drop to the bottom. Just like the roller coaster, the sea trough was waiting for the boat to make the drop. The impact might be strong enough to shatter and rip the boat apart. She was petrified. As she waited for the inevitable, she tried to see what was happening to Chris. The bow was now at the crest of the wave.

At that instant, Chris was trying to take a step, which he never completed. The upward thrust of the ascent was so powerful that it prevented any forward motion. He was violently tossed backward toward the stern. She saw Chris spinning and twisting awkwardly across the deck. She couldn't tell if his safety line held or if he was thrown overboard. As she was trying to see what was happening to Chris, the boat was now in position to start the steep decent downward. When the boat smacked into the bottom of the trough, she was hurled back into the galley where she was tossed about just like she had envisioned in her most serious moments of seasickness. She was in the spin cycle of a washing machine.

Despite the ricocheting and spinning as she was being tossed from one side of the boat to the other, she remained conscious. She expected to have some fractures or at least some bleeding, but that was not the case. After lying there for a short while, she determined that she was not physically injured. She slowly and cautiously stood up. She wanted to see what had happened to Chris. It was easier to stand than she expected because the dips of the troughs returned to three – to four-foot drops. She started making her way to the top of the galley stairwell. She double-checked to see if her safety line was still attached. It was. She also made a mental note how thankful she was that the boat did not rip apart or sink. She was sure that one or the other would happen.

Now on the top step, she was able to see that Chris had not been swept overboard, but nearly. She was not sure what had happened, but he was now in a life-threatening situation. He was on his back about twelve to thirteen feet from her and looked unconscious. Possibly dead. His safety line was still attached to his vest, but somehow it had also become tangled around his ankle. His head was at the edge of the deck on the port side just above the water. The rest of his body was in a horizontal position with his feet pointed to the starboard side. His body reacted to the turbulence of sea and the movement of the boat, which was considerable. He would flop and bounce about just like the fish that had accidentally been tossed onto the deck by the sea. It wiggled and flopped about until Chris had kicked it overboard. Chrystal was not sure what to do.

A cold and calculating thought was gaining traction. Everything that had happened was accidental. If she did nothing, she could live with a clear conscience because his tragic death would be caused by the storm. As she looked at him with that thought racing through her mind, she thought she heard a raspy, gurgling sound. Was that Chris trying to say something? She did not want to acknowledge that she might have heard a sound coming from Chris. She ignored it, turned, and went below.

Now belowdecks, Chrystal started doing some soul searching. She was having a question and answer session with herself.

"Is he alive?"

"I'm not sure, but I think I did hear a sound he made."

"Maybe I didn't really hear anything."

"The storm makes it impossible to do much."

"I'm too weak to help him. Right?"

"If I don't try to do something, it's like killing him."

"He deserves it."

"But it's unconscionable to do nothing. I couldn't live with that."

"But he deserves it."

The back and forth of the "Q and A" continued for a short while and ended abruptly when she tightened her safety line, picked up an additional safety line and the butcher knife, and headed topside.

Chrystal went back to the last step of galley stairwell and could see Chris being jostled about as his body moved with the rhythm of the boat, which was being strongly buffeted by the storm surge and the pelting rain. She still could not determine if he was dead or alive. His head was less than ten to twelve feet from where she was standing with her back to the strong wind. Under these conditions, it seemed like a city block. She was now totally committed to getting him off the deck. If successful, she'd figure out what she had to do next. She kept saying to herself that time honored English saying, "In for a penny, in for a pound." She's in for a pound. She prepared to make her move toward the kidnapper and rapist.

The deck was very slippery because of the water from the constant rain as well as saltwater that splashed over the sides. Chrystal analyzed the deck conditions and quickly decided that it would be unsafe to walk. She'd crawl. Before actually moving, she studied the boat's reaction to the troughs. She decided to be as safe as possible and try to move forward when the boat rose with the wave and then try hold her position when it dipped down the trough. She was scared but resolute. The boat nosed up the side of a three to four foot wave, and at that instant, she pushed off from the galley step. Her safety line was taut and she trusted it. She was now in a prone position and her face was maybe an inch or two above the deck surface. With the rise and fall of each wave, she got closer to Chris. Another wave, another foot. It seemed like a lifetime to reach Chris, but it was less than six or seven minutes. She reached out and grabbed the lifeline that somehow got twisted around his ankle. As she rested, she reminded herself, *now for the hard part.*

Chrystal had a decision to make. If he was alive, she would try to get him to the galley. If he was dead, she would opt for either cutting him lose with the kitchen knife she brought with her or leave him where he was until the storm is over. Over the noise of the howling wind and the sound of the rain pelting down on them, she yelled as loudly as possibly could.

"Chris, can you hear me?" She yelled several times more. He did not respond. She crawled closer to his face. There was blood near his temple. His skin was pale white with what looked like some blue coloring setting in. His eyes were open and his pupils were looking upward at his forehead. He looked dead. Chrystal screamed at him to make a sound or say something. She slapped his face. Nothing. She slapped him again only harder. Nothing. To be sure if he was dead or alive, she put her ear to his nose and mouth and listened. Because of the sounds from the wind and rain, she could not be sure if she'd be able to detect any response. He had on too many clothes, and in the harsh conditions of the moment, she could not try to check for a heartbeat. She decided there was nothing else she could do, so she removed her face from his and decided to cut his lifeline and let him fall into the sea.

Chrystal removed the knife from her clothing and grabbed his lifeline. With considerable difficulty, she started sawing on the line. She heard something that made her stop slicing the line. It was a deep guttural rasping sound. She looked at his face. His pupils seemed to move. She grabbed him by his shoulders and shook him. His eyes blinked. She now knew that he was alive. With every ounce of strength she had, she managed to roll him over. She straddled his body and started pushing on his back. There was plenty of water on the deck, but now there was more. Saltwater spewed out of his mouth. All the options of what do now narrowed down to one. Get him off the deck and get him below.

All the elements of the storm continued on, unabated. Chrystal was so focused on what she was doing that she blocked out the rolling and rocking, the trough ride, the relentless rain, the power and noise of the thunder and lightning. She fixated on one thing at a time. First, attach the lifeline she brought for Chris's jacket and attach it to where he initially clipped his line to the boat. This required that she had to crawl and shimmy her way back to the galley. As she was going through this process, she was upset with herself for not clipping on the backup line when she first set off to check on him. "I can't fret over that now," she told herself. Despite the weather and all the energy she had used, she managed to get the six-foot line attached. He was now tethered at both ends. He was safe from sliding overboard. Now she was able to cut the line that was wrapped around his ankle. She was exhausted. She also had some doubt if she had the strength and wherewithal to drag him back to the galley. There was only one way to find out, and that is exactly what she decided to do. Get his limp, heavy body off the deck.

To those unfamiliar with sailing, a forty – to forty-five foot sailboat may seem to be a good size boat, and in some regards it is. Chrystal and her family were not a boating family, and the few times she sailed as a guest, that was her impression as well. Over the last several weeks of her imprisonment, she had developed a different perspective regarding the size of Chris's boat. It was small. As she looked at the distance back to the galley, she knew it was only eight to ten steps away, but it looked like a hundred steps. Now if felt like a big boat. *It is what it is, so get going and do the best you can*, she told herself. She grabbed Chris's lifeline near his solar plexus and prepared herself mentally on how to start the retreat to the finish line—the galley.

Chrystal wasn't sure what the best way was to start this lifesaving trek. She immediately discarded the idea that she could stand up and carry or drag him the distance necessary. The sea was still very angry and its fury was zeroed in on the boat. Deductive reasoning concluded that whatever approach she tried should be in a prone position.

The safety lines were doing their job. They were well secured and short enough that she had no fear of being flipped off the boat. The idea that they might tear and sever did cross her mind, but she quickly dismissed that possibility. She had total confidence in their strength. Chris was still on his stomach. She straddled his body and rested while she tried to decide how she could move him. During this "rest," she had to come up with a realistic plan. Something that might work if she worked fast. Her strength was ebbing and she knew it. She remained bent over and looking down at Chris's back in an effort to avoid the raindrops that felt like pellets peppering her. She decided that if and when she started moving him, she wanted him to be on his back. She had no idea what he weighed. What she did know is that he was dead weight and he would be of no help getting him rolled over on his back.

As she studied the boat as it listed back and forth, she noted that there was a lot of momentum when the boat lurched in either direction. To try and take advantage of this phenomenon, she would push him, with all her might, in the direction that the boat was listing. She stopped straddling him and positioned herself on the starboard side and waited for the boat to list to the port side. Her waiting and planning paid off. When the boat rolled hard to port, she had her arms under his body and pushed during the roll. He was now face up and being pounded by the rain. She did not want him face down during the time she would be pushing or pulling him to the cabin because of the potential harm and injury that might take place. She had no idea how long it would take to accomplish what she was trying to do, so time was a serious consideration. A more serious concern was the affect the hard and continuous bouncing of the boat would have on his face and head as it smashed into the deck over and over again. Neither choice was good, but he had to be moved or he would die just a few feet from safety.

Chrystal knew it was too dangerous to stand. She decided to try and pull him by his feet. She positioned herself between his body and the galley entrance. Now hunched over and on her knees, she grabbed each foot and awkwardly tried to back up as she pulled him in the direction of the cabin. Her partially erect body was immediately slammed by the wind causing her to lose her grip of Chris's feet. She and Chris were sent sprawling across the deck, but to only the length of the safety line. Six feet. When they jerked to a stop, they were less than a foot from the edge of the boat. Chrystal was now on top of Chris who was still on his back, face up. She was shaken up, but not deterred. Her adrenaline flowed as she lay there trying to figure out what she would do next.

She took a few seconds to reevaluate the situation. The strong wind with gusts up to forty to fifty miles per hour, plus the constant and severe pitching and listing of the boat, ruled out standing or, as she just learned, partial standing. "What's left?" she asked herself.

"Stay low and crawl." Mentally strong but physically weakening, she'd try one more time to get them back to the galley. An unwanted thought crossed her mind. "I hope I'm not dealing with a dead body."

Shimmying backward, she inched herself off of Chris but still remained prone. When she got to her feet, she once again grabbed each of Chris's feet. Using her elbows and knees, she would try to move him by moving backward a few inches at a time. She would wait until the sea was between troughs before she tried. Her stomach was flat on the surface of the deck. The rain and the saltwater from the sea continued to flow across the deck as the boat listed back and forth. She had to be careful not to swallow any of the water as it passed under her mouth and nose, which was only two or three inches above the deck surface. Before she actually tried to move the barely conscious Chris, she looked at him, and it wasn't a pretty sight. He was being pelted by the rain and the saltwater that splashed over the sides. He looked terrible. She looked away. It was now time to start her backward retreat to the cabin. She started pulling on his feet as she squirmed and wiggled to get some traction and get him off the deck. A major problem developed. She couldn't budge him. He was too heavy and she didn't have the strength to move him.

Stymied but still resolute, she tried to come up with a way to solve this unexpected problem. She reflected on what she had done to get Chris rolled over. After some reflection and evaluation, she decided that her idea on how to move him was the wrong approach. She had resisted the motions of the boat and tried to hold her ground as she and Chris were jostled about. She had been holding on either a stainless steel line, or a cleat, or a block for the ropes, or anything else she could reach, so they could remain in place. Why not use the motion of boat to help her once again? When the boat traveled up and then down the troughs, she would use the boat's momentum to help her. When the boat slid over the crest of a wave and then plunged downward, they would both slide toward the cabin. It was like a playground slide. It was also like a teeter-totter. Up and down. She had no idea how much area might be gained or lost. It didn't matter. Her theory was about to be tested.

A decently sized wave was forming, and the bow was now on the ascent. She let go of the cleat she was holding on to, got on top of Chris, and waited for the slide. She waited and waited. It was not as large as she thought. The bow of the boat gently eased over the wave. There was no deep, rapid drop. She was surprised and somewhat disappointed. The large waves she had anticipated did not develop. She was almost afraid to think that the storm was starting to end, but she truly hoped and prayed that was the case. Just to be sure that the sea was losing its power and calming down, she decided to hang on to Chris and wait awhile longer. She was itching to get him below deck and find out if he was dead or alive. *Wait until you are sure what to do.* So she waited.

The boat's motion was stabilizing and the wind was losing its power. She got off of Chris so she could determine if there was enough slack in the line to allow her to partially stand up and start the herculean task of dragging him to the cabin entrance. She was able to stand, but only in a crouched position. There was enough line to allow her to walk backward and hopefully get the seemingly lifeless body to slide across the deck. It was time to move. She took the first step. She moved him about six inches. That little bit of movement gave her a dash of euphoria. She felt like she had just crossed the finish line in a hundred yard dash and she was the winner. There were no cheers, no accolades, just personal satisfaction. She readied her body for backward step two. Using as much leverage as possible, she pulled and tugged with all her might and succeeded in getting him to the cabin entrance, six inches at a time.

Chrystal was exhausted. She had to stop any further physical exertion and rest before she attempted to get Chris down the steep stairwell. During this pause, she was heartened as she looked at the horizon and saw the sun. It was like a huge gold nugget that sparkled and glistened as it started to erase the gloomy darkness of the storm. The sparkle of the blue skies and ocean were starting to return. The horizon of dark clouds was now being replaced by white ones. It was uplifting and it raised her spirits. She now felt strong enough to tackle the last obstacle: the stairs.

The boat was still pitching and listing, but compared to what she had experienced over the past few days, the boat's movement would not be a problem. She still had her safety line attached to Chris's vest and decided the best way to lower him was to keep her line attached to him and slowly ease him down to the cabin floor. She began to lower him feet first. Since her line was snapped to his vest, she would be able control the rate of lowering by leaning slightly backward with each cautious step she took. The agonizingly slow process ended with Chris safely on the floor and an emotionally and physically exhausted Chrystal laying on top of him. She couldn't move. She didn't want to move. Sobbing she uttered, "I did it, I did it." Reality forced her to take the next step. She unlatched the safety lines and started removing his vest and jacket. She laid her head on his chest and listened. She thought she heard a very faint sound. She did. He had a heartbeat.

CHAPTER 29

The cabin was warm and dry. Chrystal had removed all his soaked clothing and covered him with a dry sheet. Several hours had passed since he was rescued, and he still had not gained consciousness. She was not too concerned about him recovering because his breathing was deeper and there were traces of coloring starting to show in his cheeks. Occasionally he would twitch, and that seemed to be occurring more frequently. She decided that realistically all she could do was wait.

The ocean was calming down and the boat was no longer rocking and bobbing as it had been for the past few days. A more tranquil setting was developing. As she watched over Chris, she started thinking about what lay ahead. She anticipated that he would ask her why she saved him. Her partially true answer would be that she could not allow a human being to perish when she had a chance to do something about it. She believed that would be an unbearable remembrance to live with. Equally and probably more accurate is that she needed him alive if she expected to escape from her forty-foot jail cell. She had to keep him off guard and bide for more time hoping that the right circumstances would develop so she could gain her freedom. She wanted him to believe that a seamanship bond had developed over the past several weeks and that influenced her to pull him to safety. As these various scenarios were spinning around in her brain, she was snapped back to the moment when she saw Chris's fingers slowly opening and closing like he was trying to make a fist. His fingers were just barely moving, but he slowly wiggled and squeezed them as if he was trying to figure out if they worked. She remained vigilant as she waited for him to wake up.

As she looked down at the quasi-unconscious rapist who she just rescued, she noticed a slight movement of his eyelids, as if he was struggling to open them. He was trying to blink, and as he did so, small slits started to appear so that the whites of his eyes began to show. Once they opened, it looked like he wanted to scream but couldn't. It was like he had been in some tranquil and peaceful setting and instantly and unexpectedly it changed to confusion, uncertainty, and danger. His eyes bulged, his lips quivered, his body shook. He was trying to yell or say something. If there was ever a face filled with terror, she was now looking at one. He didn't yell, he screamed. "Chrystal! Chrystal!"

Chrystal knelt by his side to comfort him. He kept staring in the direction of the small kitchen at the cork stingrays she had crafted earlier in her imprisonment. When she made them, she knew they were crude in appearance and their features were exaggerated. The tails were too long, the eyes too big, they were too wide. She didn't care. She hung them up and Chris never removed them. For some inexplicable reason, their image triggered how he reacted. Perhaps it was like when a person is having a terrible dream and it won't end. The only way to end the nightmare is force yourself to wake up. In this case, it could have been the opposite. He was having wonderful thoughts in a Camelot-like setting and didn't want to wake up.

"Chris, you are okay. You're safe. There is nothing to be afraid of. Wake up."

He looked at Chrystal and then his eyes scanned the cabin. As his orientation increased, his fear and uncertainty started to ease. Chrystal could tell he was trying to say something. His first post-traumatic experience comment was twofold. He spoke. "I can't believe I am alive. Chrystal, are we still moving south?"

"You're very much alive, and I have no idea if we are going south," she responded.

"Go look and tell me the location of the sun."

She stood on the top stair and checked, then yelled down, "it's kind of on the right side."

"That's good. We're still going in the right direction. The sea anchor must have helped."

Chrystal returned to the cabin and sat near Chris. He was obviously very tired and needed time to recover from the physical beating he had just endured. In a maternal way, she suggested he rest and they could talk later. He nodded in agreement. With Chrystal's help, he walked to the bed and lay down. As Chrystal started to walk away, he said, "We might have a real problem. I found out the metal object that was being flung about in the storm broke the compass." It stopped her in her tracks. She equated "no compass" to being lost. It was sad and depressing news. She needed fresh air and time to think. She headed topside.

A warm tropical breeze greeted her once she left the galley. She was too upset to appreciate how pleasant the gentle air should have felt. She arranged a couple vinyl cushions and sat down. Sitting there, a deep depression started to seep into her psyche. She never felt more alone than at this very moment. She looked at the vastness of the ocean and it only increased her loneliness and feelings of despair. She felt like just giving up on any plan or hope of surviving. She had been through so much and managed to survive, but being lost at sea was something that she never considered. She could end it all by leaping over the side of the boat, right now, and watch the boat continue southward without her. In a few minutes, her pain and suffering would end. In those moments of reflection, the thought occurred to her that there was one word Chris used when he broke the news about having no compass. He said it "might" be a problem. Maybe it was significant, maybe not, but it gave her a ray of hope that there was possibility that Chris knew an alternative way to navigate. She adopted a new enthusiasm and appreciation for the word "might." With her spirits lifted somewhat, she decided that there was nothing else she could do at the moment, so she spent the rest of the day working on the boat and retired to the galley for the evening.

During the night hours, the sea steadily calmed and had a slight north to south breeze. Chrystal was quite surprised when shafts of sunlight splashed across her face and woke her up. She looked over at Chris, and he was resting comfortably. To make sure he was okay, she gently shook him until he woke up. He was still groggy, but slowly opened his eyes. After a few minutes, he was alert. He said he felt much better. It was amazing how fast both of them were recuperating from yesterday's experience. Their youth contributed greatly to their ability to rebound so quickly. Now awake, Chrystal could not wait to talk about having no compass and the possibility that they were now lost and what, if anything, could be done about it.

"Chris, are you going to be able to find land someplace with no compass? We desperately need water, food, and gas."

He had a most serious look on his young face. He stared straight ahead at nothing. "Chrystal, in all honesty, I'm not sure what I can do. I'll think about it. I hope I can, but I am not optimistic."

After hearing that rather depressing answer, she left him alone and went to the bow of the boat. She liked this spot. She could look at the entire length of the boat as well as the wake that followed. This morning, doom permeated the atmosphere. As she sat there depressed, her mind wandered and touched on various topics. One such topic was her ability to utilize her high school French if the occasion should ever occur. She hoped that someday she'd get that chance, but now it looked more and more doubtful. So, she sat there with one leg crossed over the other and her head in her hands staring at the zigzagging wake trailing behind the boat. The pattern seemed to symbolize what lay ahead. Confusion.

CHAPTER 30

Chris was now alone with his thoughts on how he might get them—mostly himself—to safety. He had no idea what to do. He just kept staring at the cabin floor hoping that some intelligent idea would develop and he could swing into action. No matter how hard he thought, nothing came to mind. Absolutely nothing. As nothingness ruled his thinking about navigation, he switched to how to save himself, and what to do about Chrystal. It was his original intention to have her for sexual pleasure, and at some point in time, she would have to be taken care of—and not in a good way. She complicated the issue by saving his life. He did make one decision. What to do about Chrystal can wait. For now, survival was the only thing on the agenda.

Unable to develop any ideas of what to do, he decided to search for anything his father might have stashed away that might help him at this critical time. He remembered his father stored numerous items under the seats that lined the port side. He stood up and removed the small thin pillows and pulled on the latch to open the wooden lid that also served as a seat. He started removing typical items you'd expect to find on sailboats. Life preservers, emergency lights, flares, and so forth. He was about to close the lid when he saw a few old pamphlets and magazines under one of the orange lifejackets. He picked them up and scanned the titles and instantly dropped all of them except one pamphlet titled "Constellation Guide in the Sky." He felt like he was holding the Hope Diamond in his hands. This magazine could be a game changer. A most fortuitous development. With just a tinge of optimism, he went topside to share the find with Chrystal.

While the sun was starting to make its daily rise, the two of them were huddled under the cockpit tarp flipping through the tarnished and aging pages of the pamphlet. Neither one had any knowledge about constellations, so the diagrams, sketches, photos (both in color and black and white), lines crisscrossing from one point to another, names, and locations of stars they had never heard of. It was a whole new world for them to learn about. Their knowledge of the sparkling diamonds in the sky was limited to spotting The Big Dipper. They both knew they had a lot to learn if this pamphlet was going to be the key that opened the door to the magic kingdom of the stars that were their companion every night. They also knew that their survival depended on the information in the aging pamphlet they held in their hands.

The majority of the day was spent reading and rereading the pamphlet and trying to decipher what was important, especially as it related to what they thought their location was. It wasn't the easiest reading for them to digest, but Chrystal was able to understand charts and graphs accurately and then explain it to Chris in more simply. The one fact that they both knew was that they had crossed the equator and were moving in a southerly direction. Other than that, they needed to rely on what was in the guide if they had any chance of reaching land. It was also obvious they must learn how to determine what constellation was the correct one to follow and hope they were right. After hours of reading and discussing what they read, they were certain they must learn how to recognize a constellation called the Southern Cross. It's a constant formation of stars that they can use to ensure they are sailing south. There were photos of the formation in color and black and white. They felt confident that they would be able to find it once it got dark and the stars were visible. All they could do now was wait for the night to make its appearance so the first class of star gazing could take place.

Chris arranged to have the boat on automatic steering and joined Chrystal at the bow. They were sitting at the very tip of the bow with their legs dangling over the side. They had a front row seat. Twilight was starting to take place, but as far they were concerned, it seemed to be getting dark agonizingly slowly. It was too early to spot stars, but they scanned the sky anyway. Looking for that first twinkle of a star, any star. So they waited with the pamphlet and flashlight at the ready.

"Chris, look, just to the right a little bit, there's a star."

"I see it," he said. The heavens were about to come alive with their nightly performance. The audience of two could hardly wait for the show to begin. It wasn't long before the sky was ablaze with stars and they were able to ferret out certain formations. There were some false sightings, which was discouraging. Perseverance paid off. Before saying anything, Chrystal studied a formation of stars that matched the material they had been studying most of the day. When she was confident of what she was looking at, she yelled, "I see it!" She showed Chris where to look. He couldn't see it at first, but Chrystal told him you have to use your imagination. "It's a cross that is tilted somewhat, and by connecting key stars, they do form a cross. Look, just like the ones in the drawings and photos." They checked and rechecked what they were looking at over and over. Everything jived. The drawings, the various photos, and what they were now looking at in the dark night sparkling with stars. The Southern Cross would become their nightly guest. They changed the formation's name to the Constellation Compass.

Chrystal couldn't stop looking at the formation of stars that were straight ahead and due south. Chris left the bow and went aft to adjust the automatic steering so the boat would continue its southward journey throughout the night. He also set the mainsail and adjusted the height just enough to catch some of the wind, which would enable them to gain a few ocean miles as they slept. After he completed his task, he went below feeling hopeful that in the days ahead, and with a lot of luck, they might actually have a chance to find one of the many islands in the Marquesas. He was satisfied that there wasn't anything else to do tonight, so he lay on the bed thinking about the difficult times that faced them. Some of the potential problems or concerns that occurred to him he'd discuss with Chrystal in the morning. Before he drifted off to sleep, the one perpetual thought that never left his mind was how and when to dispose of the woman topside. It was a disturbing thought, but he knew he had to do something, and he would.

Chrystal was in no hurry to leave the bow. It was a warm tropical evening and the light warm breeze that wafted from bow to aft felt good. Her eyes rarely left the sight of the star formation she had found earlier. It was like there was a laser beam between her and the cross.

It was her beacon of hope. A good omen. Perhaps a step in helping her to end this nightmare. She pleaded with the stars, "Show me the way to escape before he kills me." She felt certain her time with Chris would probably end in death. Her mind was in a constant vortex of fright and nerves. Despite the problematic likelihood she'd survive, she still planned to escape if the right set of circumstances should develop. As she sat there doing mental gymnastics about her situation, she felt a surge of mental fatigue setting in, so she headed back to the cabin and bed. She hoped Chris would be asleep and not touch her.

CHAPTER 31

When Chrystal woke up, she did not immediately get out of bed. She reflected on the good fortune of finding the pamphlet and the Southern Cross yesterday. There had been very few good things that had happened on the "boat ride from hell," but now, at least, one positive development had occurred. Now, with some certainty, they would know of true direction as they sailed. Chris started to wake. That was her signal to quietly, but quickly, slip out her side of the bed to avoid any unwelcomed physical contact with the man she saved, yet despised.

The sea was calm and there was enough wind to keep the boat moving in a southern direction, so it was a quiet time for her. She looked over at Chris and he had fallen back to sleep. She decided to look at some of the other pamphlets and books they discovered. One of the small books was titled The Archipelago of the Pacific, or the sea of many islands. She flipped through a few pages looking at maps, diagrams, and pictures. Since she was one of the forced denizens of the Pacific Ocean, she started reading and memorizing salient things that now interested her. What she was reading gave her additional hope for survival. The vastness of the ocean had been one of the major factors causing her to be depressed and have feelings of hopelessness. Now, maybe, just maybe, there was a positiveness within the pages she was reading. So she read with great interest about the size and number of islands that hopefully they would see in their southern sail.

There were some muffled sounds coming from the direction of the bed. Chrystal looked over and saw that Chris was trying to wake up. He reached over to her side of the bed and felt about. Touching nothing but the sheet, he rolled over on his side to examine why. No Chrystal, no sex. Now awake, he could see her in the galley and see she had a book.

"What are you reading?" he asked.

"About the archipelago that lies ahead. Lots of info that we need to study. Come over here and let's read the material together." Before he completed the four or five steps to where she was sitting, his barista background tried to kick in. He visualized sipping a latte to start his day, not reading a book. The image of a cup of coffee quickly vanished. Any drink other than their daily ration of water was not possible.

"Can't waste the water," he mumbled to himself. Without anything to drink, he sat next to her and said, "Let's see what ya got."

The highlight of the data for both of them was the vastness that the Marquesas and Society Islands covered. An expanse of over 1,200 miles. Equally significant was the 118 islands within that radius. There was an asterisk by the number of islands quoted that advised the reader that there were numerous small islands called motus that were uninhabited and not included in the island count. The size of the target area was huge. It was uplifting information and it boosted their morale.

"Okay, Chrystal, let's go topside and start the search for one of those 118."

Standing at the helm with some assurance that the bow was slicing through the water in a southern position was a comforting feeling. Chris, however, had some reservations and concerns about staying on a strict north-to-south steerage. Chrystal turned to the page with the map that showed the United States and Tahiti.

"Doesn't a straight southern line look like we might be too far east of the islands we hope to find?" She studied the map and believed that could be the case. "We could sail right by those islands and not even know it."

After some thought, Chris suggested that in the evening, once they see the Southern Cross constellation, they could set the automatic steering on a southwesterly tack. The bow would still be aimed at "the cross," but with a minor correction—the North Star would always be behind the boat.

"If we do that, I think we will have a better chance of bumping into one of the islands. So let's sail on and hope Lady Luck will be with us. In the meantime, will you go and check on our food and water supply and come back. Then we will talk some more."

The initial jubilation started to wane the more Chris thought about how to navigate without a compass and the physical demands the sail ahead would require. He was in deep thought when Chrystal returned.

"Okay, here's what food and water we have on hand. Do you want me to tell you what food items we have?"

"No, just give your opinion on how long we could survive with what we have."

"If we really skimp, maybe ten days, two weeks tops."

"Okay, how about the water?"

"Thanks to the way we trapped rainwater during the storm and how we have rationed how much water we drink every day, the water will last about the same time as the food."

"Okay that tells me the time frame we have to deal with as we try to find land." The serious look on his face and his body language transmitted a clear message that he wanted to be alone. He said nothing more. It was obvious he didn't want to talk anymore, so Chrystal left him and went to the bow, her usual spot when she wanted to be left alone. She spent a lot of time there.

It was a long day. It seemed like the daylight fought gallantly to fend off the darkness of the night, but for millennia, they both took their turn every twenty-four hours. Dusk slowly started to arrive, and on this clear night, both of them waited for their beacon of hope to show its cross of stars. They were not disappointed. Like an operatic diva, the Southern Cross took the stage. Chris immediately adjusted the rudder so that the bow was now headed right at the formation. Once that was done, the boat was set on autopilot. The main and jib sails were in place and capturing the wind as they sailed southwest.

Chrystal and Chris sat silently in the helm watching as the night and its perpetual guests created a magnificent, sparkling, diamond-studded sky. Their minds were on two totally different topics. Chrystal wondered what Chris's last name was and if Chris really is his name. When she asked him, he'd always say "call me Chris." She eventually quit asking him about it. Chris on the other hand was thinking if they could survive with the amount of food and water they had, plus navigation uncertainty. Chris broke the silence.

"Chrystal, I think if we stay on the current course, we will be too far east and will miss the islands of the Marquesas. If I'm right, we need to constantly adjust our course somewhat to the west. The archipelagos cover such a large area that I feel we'd have a decent chance of spotting an island if we continue to tack in a southwesterly direction, as I have said before. So that's what we will try and hope for the best." With that said, he adjusted the course of the boat in the direction he suggested.

Chrystal was completely aware that she had no control on how they sailed, so she offered no comment, but she did have one question.

"What do you think the distance is that we have to sail to reach the Marquesas Islands?"

Chris thought about the question and eventually said, "I'd guess around a thousand miles." The distance he estimated was shocking. She started calculating how many miles a day they would have to sail to approach that number and she wasn't happy with how the math worked out. It was depressing. An analogy crossed her mind. Now, she could appreciate how a person could feel after a doctor tells them they have just so many days to live. In her current situation, the "Doctor of Reality" had just told her she had two weeks to live, unless Chris intervened. She walked to her sanctuary, the bow, and stood facing in the direction of the Southern Cross. In her mind, it started to take a different shape. It was morphing into a crucifix as if some power of the universe was telling her not to give up. Don't quit. It was a powerful illusion. She vowed to not give up. Her mantra was, *I'll make it even if Chris doesn't.*

CHAPTER 32

Chris remained at the helm the entire night keeping the boat on a south-west tack. It was his plan to sail in the direction of the cross and adjust the direction from time to time with a sharp tack west and then line up again on the Southern Cross. He would repeat this throughout the night. Being completely honest with himself, he knew that the odds were not in their favor to come upon an island, but it was the only viable thing he could think of, so he sailed on. He tired of second-guessing himself and ended his constant worry about his plan with the thought that at least he had one. He settled in on the routine of keeping the boat into the wind and on course. The wind had been favorable and the luffing and flapping of the sails was minimal, so he was able to sail an optimum distance throughout the night without constantly adjusting the sails. He felt that the first night of sailing to the "sea of islands" was a good one.

Below in the cabin, Chrystal fixated on the time remaining before something surly had to happen during the remaining days left on this frightening and now dangerous boat ride. Her original plan, if the right set of circumstances developed, was still firmly in place and she would not deviate from it. Her mind bounced from one idea to another searching for a secondary plan to hopefully ensure her safety. She rejected idea after idea. She could not think of any intelligent or plausible alternative to her original scheme, so fate and Lady Luck would now be in charge. Before she went topside to relieve Chris who had pulled the night shift at the helm, a couple thoughts crossed her mind. Since Chris had basically assigned her the role of rationing out the daily food and water, she would try to set aside a little extra for herself. She would need all her strength if the opportunity arose to escape. If he found her cache, she would explain that she had done so with their best interest in mind pointing out to him that if after ten to twelve days passed and he felt like giving up, she would have some extra sustenance so they could hang on a little longer. She accepted the fact that there were risks involved but felt she could get him to accept her explanation. For the moment, she put aside her machinations and headed for the stairs. As was her habit over the past several days, she glanced in the direction of the sink to make sure the butcher knife was still on the rack. She hoped she'd never have to use it, or have it used on her.

During the next five or six days, the weather conditions were constant, and for the most part, they were able to maintain an acceptable speed of five to seven knots per hour for extended periods of time. Their bodies were showing the effects of minimum food and water. They were tired. It was difficult to be optimistic. Day and night, they constantly scanned the horizon for any sight of that would remotely suggest there was anything else to see other than the ocean. The likelihood that the sailing tack they were on would be successful was fading day by day. Both were getting depressed. Their bodies were weakened to the extent that the smallest task was difficult to do. At times, dizziness occurred as well as hallucinations where both of them thought they saw birds or lights in the distance. Reality would snap in and that dash of excitement would vanish. Pessimism was slipping into despair and hopelessness. They rarely talked. It used up energy, which they had little of. Chrystal, now at the helm, watched Chris walk to the cabin. His shoulders were hunched as he cautiously made his way to the cabin. He was in his twenties, yet he walked like he was in the last days of his life. She thought, *I hope I don't look like that, but maybe I do.* She looked away and started doing what she had been doing for weeks—looking for land.

As Chrystal scanned the skies, she saw what was no hallucination. A squall was heading their way from the west. She left the helm and made sure all the various ways she used to trap water during the major storm were in place to receive the liquid gold that would soon arrive. She perceived the darkening skies as a good omen. When the first drops kissed her face, she licked her lips. It tasted fantastic. Her spirits were like the stock market—they were spiking up fast, and she was enjoying every second of it. Her fervent wish was that the rain would last long enough to accumulate as much water as possible. Her wish was granted. It rained all morning and into the early afternoon.

Both of Chris's hands were trembling as he lifted the cup of water Chrystal had brought to him. The wonderful taste of the rainwater was beyond description. He felt like his heart had stopped beating and the doctor had just activated an electrical shock treatment and his lifeless body returned to the here and now. She left the cabin because she heard the sails luffing and needed to make the necessary adjustment to keep the bow into the wind. Now, with a modicum of rejuvenation, he decided to join Chrystal topside. In a few hours, it would be his turn to relieve her at the helm, so he decided to enjoy the remaining hour or two of daylight in the helm. The storm passed and a sunset was starting to develop in the western skies. It was a beautiful sunset. As the day slowly started to phase into dusk, the quiet and solitude of the moment was suddenly interrupted when Chrystal leaped to her feet and pointed southwest.

"Chris, look over there. There's a bird—no, two birds. Do you see them?"

"I do, I do!" he said.

The sight of the birds had two distinctive reactions from the two of them. Chrystal hoped land was nearby and it would give her a chance to escape the nightmare she'd endured for so many weeks. Chris, on the other hand, wanted to avoid contact with people. That could greatly influence Chrystal's continued existence. Both reflecting on their private thoughts, they remained at the helm during the night vigilantly looking for any sign of land. It was very dark. They were tense.

Simultaneously, they saw a light that was not a star. They were sailing on a direct line toward it. Chrystal's pulse was racing with excitement. She cautioned herself to not be too demonstrative. Chris's mood was subdued, but outwardly pretending to be glad. He wasn't that sure which mood should prevail.

Their course was now locked in on the light as the night started to give way to the morning light. They had no way to tell time, so the position of the sun was how they gauged the approximate time of the day. The sun was overhead by the time they neared the island surrounded by coral. With about three hours of daylight left, they sailed around the island looking for a pathway through the reef so they could enter the lagoon. Some islands have more than one entrance to the lagoon. This island had just one. With about an hour of daylight left, they located the passageway to the island. They started their approach to the entrance of the lagoon, which they entered without a problem. The open sea was now behind them, and they were in quiet water.

CHAPTER 33

The mainsail had been lowered. The thirty-five mile per hour motor was now in charge of the forward motion of the boat as it slowly moved toward a location within the lagoon. Chris was very selective in where he decided to stay for the evening. He eventually picked a spot that was some distance from the shoreline. A rather isolated and remote area. No buildings or people in the immediate area. Chrystal thought they were less than a mile from the where a few homes were located. It was obviously a very small community with very few people living there. What was of paramount importance to her was that it was an inhabited motu. It was a serene and tranquil setting that she hoped to become a part of in the next twenty-four hours. If she didn't, it would be because she was no longer alive. She vowed that under no circumstances would she leave the lagoon a captive of Chris.

By the time the boat was anchored, it was almost dark. What would happen tonight? Whatever happened, if anything, she would stay alert and fight to the death if she had to. She had her guard up and constantly watched him as he moved about. She had removed the butcher knife from the holder and placed it where she could reach it fast if he tried anything in the cabin. She was intense but tried to act nonchalant. Chris was topside and called for her to join him. It was a call that terrified her. *Is this the time he will choke me out like he did with the chloroform? Will he try to knock me out or strangle me?* She was nervous and scared. The stairwell out of the cabin looked like the steps to climb to the gallows. She slowly took each step like it could be the last time she'd do so. Chris was sitting on the top of the cabin and pointed at the bright light they spotted at sea.

"That's our savior. Without that light, I don't think we would have made it. Wonderful sight, huh?"

"Indeed," she said." After a slight pause, she asked, with considerable trepidation, "What are we going to do tomorrow?"

"I don't know. Well talk about it tomorrow."

That response was priceless. It gave her a window of time to do what she had to do. "Okay, sounds good." She was squirming and itching to do what she had planned since the first few days of her captivity.

There are situations and times when the minutes and hours seem to stand still. For Chrystal, that was taking place now. She wanted him in bed and asleep. After what seemed an eternity, she faked tiredness and told Chris that she was really looking forward to a peaceful night's sleep in the quiet water of the lagoon. She went below and waited. She dreaded the thought and was irritated with herself for thinking that she might be the one who would initiate a sexual evening, but was more than willing to do so if it helped her be successful in her escape. *Keep him happy and tired.* So she waited. She also had placed the cold, razor-sharp butcher knife under her side of the thin mattress. She heard him moving about on the deck and walking in the direction of the cabin steps.

Chris entered the bed. Chrystal was completely successful in her effort to exhaust him by using her femininity and sexuality to induce fatigue and the need for him to recover physically. Now on her side of the small bed, she looked over at him. He was panting, sweating, and breathing hard as he took deep gulps of breath and then exhaled slowly trying to recover from the blissful sexual experience that just took place. Chrystal considered it disgusting, but necessary. She turned off the small dim light and waited some more. For weeks they had been sleeping in the same bed, so she could tell when he was in a deep sleep. She had to remind herself not to act too soon. When she was sure he was sound asleep, she slowly, with the stealth of a lion approaching its prey, eased out of the bed and out of the cabin. She clutched the knife as she did so.

Chris rolled over on his side and reached out to touch Chrystal, but she wasn't there. It woke him up. She must be topside. He drifted back to sleep. He had no idea how much time had elapsed, but once again, in a sleepy stupor, he casually reached out to touch her. She was not there. Concerned, he got out of bed and headed for the stairwell. Standing on the top step, he looked from the bow to the stern. There was a half-moon shining, so he was able to see the entire boat in less than three seconds. He was immediately convinced she was not on the boat. To be absolutely sure, he did a quick walkabout. The walk confirmed his suspicions. She was gone!

The events of the last few minutes caused Chris to panic. He quickly reasoned that she had to be in the water. He knew she was a terrible swimmer. During the trip and when they stopped to cool off or wash their bodies in the ocean, she stayed very close to him. She held on to the rope they used for security with a death grip. She confessed that she was not a good swimmer. If she was trying to get to shore, he was certain that she'd never make it. He ran to the Zodiac to inflate it and get it in the water. It was then he saw the butcher knife. She had used it to slash the rubber inflatable boat in several places making it useless. The symbolism of the knife and the slashes dropped him to his knees. He felt like he had been in a boxing match and the fight was stopped because he could not continue. He was defeated.

Chris slowly walked to the cabin. During the few steps he took, he kept stepping on pieces of cork. He couldn't make any sense of the cork being on the deck. It didn't matter. He had to do something, and quickly. With all the power and money that her family had, they would be able to use numerous resources to find her. He had to leave the lagoon immediately. He did not know when Chrystal left the boat, nor did he know if she made it to land or if she was alive. It was time to go topside and hoist the anchor and head to the open sea. For some inexplicable reason, he noticed that the ugly and oversized stingrays Chrystal had made using cork were gone. He wondered if she had taken them as a reminder and a souvenir of her time and experience on the boat. He didn't care. He started the engines and headed for the outlet of the lagoon. The first hint of daylight could be seen on the horizon. He looked back at the small village and wondered if she made it. He hoped she did not.

CHAPTER 34

As Chrystal left the cabin, she gently removed the cork stingrays she had made earlier in her confinement and, armed with the knife, she cautiously and quietly made her way to the aft part of the boat. There was a very dim, bluish light that shone during the night in the area where the compass had been broken. She used the light to alter the appearance and configuration of her crude works of art. She had designed a set of swim fins by using old rug remnants she had found in one of the storage cabinets. She outlined her foot size on the carpet and then cut the rug to the dimension she had drawn. She removed a lot of the fuzz from the rug and then applied the small pieces of cork. She used two pieces of rug for each foot to create a pouch effect then used fishing line to sew them together. She was careful to strengthen a point in the fin so that later when she opened the pouch and slipped her foot in, it would not unravel. The tail of the stingray was two pieces of leather cut into strips and lashed together with twine. Her plan was to cut the twine lengthwise and then use the strips to secure the improvised fins to her ankles. Before she entered the water, she would scrape off some of the cork because she did not want them to be too buoyant. She methodically started the reconfiguration process, and in less than five minutes, she had them strapped to her feet and was ready to swim to shore. After slashing the inflatable boat, she slipped into the water. A quote from a civil rights activist came to mind as she took her first stroke to freedom, "Free, free, at last."

Chrystal had absolutely no fear or doubt that she could swim to the distant shore. During her college days, she met an exchange student from France. Joachim Blanchet, a well-known long-distance swimmer. He introduced her to swimming as a way to unwind from the rigors of academia. She became proficient as she swam various distances and continued doing so after she graduated from college. She would now put into practice what he taught her.

Reach out on each stroke. Take long strokes. Do not breathe on each stroke. She had also calculated that the tide was coming in and that would be helpful. She believed that she could make the swim by morning light, even in her weakened physical condition. Chrystal was particularly proud of how she had deceived Chris by pretending that swimming was like a near-death experience for her. She was also pleased that the rug fins, so far, were holding up. Freedom and rescue were an hour away.

A local fisherman slowly eased his boat into his favorite area of the lagoon to fish. He turned off his small fifteen mile per hour engine and allowed the boat to drift as he prepared his fishing line with some bait. His habit was to fish almost every morning at day's first light. Satisfied that the bait was firmly attached to the hook and he had the proper weight attached to the line, he raised the pole to cast. As he did so, his eye detected something that made him stop. He put the pole down and stared hard at the shoreline. He didn't want to believe what his eyes and brain were suggesting. He started his engine and slowly moved closer to shore to get a better look. When he was about two hundred yards away from the beach, he confirmed that indeed there was a person lying face down in the sand at the water's edge. Less than a hundred people live on the island so he should know who it was, but he knew instantly that he did not know this person because of the white skin. Nobody lived on Raraka aside from Tahitians, and no people with white skin. He moved closer to shore.

"*Sacrebleu*, it's a lady." He threw his anchor over the side and waded in the shallow water to her.

The fisherman, Etera Amaru, initially thought the lady might be dead or just barely alive. He wasn't sure. He picked up her limp unresponsive body, put her in his boat, and headed for the small cluster of homes fifteen minutes away. There were no medical facilities or personnel on the island, so he took her to his home. His wife, Ete, had the reputation as someone to go to in an emergency. The TLC they provided was successful. Slowly, Chrystal's body began to show signs of life as she slowly blinked and then opened her eyes. After a few sips of tea, she realized that she was in a safe environment. She asked if they spoke English. "No," was their instant response. She hoped she could remember enough French to communicate with her saviors.

"S'il vous plaît téléphoner à la gendarmerie." That was about the best she could think of to put across the point that she needed help from the police. They nodded they understood.

There was no airport on the remote island of Raraka. Two days after Chrystal was found on the beach, the police arrived on the island on a high-powered speedboat to investigate and evaluate the status of Chrystal. She identified who she was and told them everything she could recall from the moment of abduction to rescue. The interrogation went on for most of the day. After hearing her story and checking on certain facts, they informed her that she would be able to contact her family before they took her back to the island of Tahiti. She was handed a phone. She dialed her home phone number.

"Hello." Chrystal could hardly talk. "Daddy."

During the powerboat trip back to the main island, she was told it would take most of the day to get there. The boat ride was uncomfortable. The sea was choppy, which caused the boat to bounce and smack the water hard as it sped over the tops of the chop. Only one of the police officers spoke any English—and not very well—so communication was limited. It gave her time to reflect on some aspects of the drama she had just lived through. At the top of the list was the fact that Chris allowed her to remain alive. If he had committed a foolproof act, as he said, why give her a chance to be anywhere near land and people? It was just the circumstances she hoped and prayed would happen. *Maybe,* she thought, *the fact I saved his life saved mine.* She had lots of "maybes" going through her mind. Maybe he did not have the stomach to deliberately take another person's life. Maybe that's it, maybe not. She'd never know.

Her reflections of the past weeks were interrupted when the police informed her that they had made arrangements to stop at an island that had an airport and they would continue the trip from there. She was told they would be at the airport in a couple hours. So Chrystal hung on to the arm-rest tightly as they bounced at a high rate of speed through the whitecapped ocean. Her mind drifted back to the swim from the boat to the shore. She had completely miscalculated her ability to make the swim that had to be close to a mile. The weeks at sea without enough food and water had weakened her far more then she thought. The rug fins she was so proud of were of little help. Ten minutes into the swim they started to fall apart. The stitching was not strong enough to offset the constant kicking.

She also quickly realized that she really was not in shape enough to take on the ambitious swim. All those factors aside, she had one powerful asset. Her determination. It's what saved her, but it almost didn't. The depth of the water near land is considerably different than California. As a general rule, the water gets deep on the Southern California beaches much sooner than the shoreline near land inside lagoons. During the last two to three hundred yards from land, Chrystal was physically spent. Her grit and determination were fading. She didn't think she'd make it. She started thinking about dying when she was so close to land. She forced one weak stroke after another telling herself not to give up. It kept getting more and more difficult to raise her arms for the next stroke. Her breathing had no rhythm as she took short breaths, actually more like gasps, just to get air. As she was fighting the battle to stay afloat, her body threatened to shut down. She could feel dizziness starting to develop as well as her ability to fight off fainting. Her body was no longer prone or on top of the water. Her legs started to drift downward. She felt herself starting to sink when divine intervention must have set in because her foot touched sand, which gave her the stimulation needed to stay conscious. From that second forward, she forced herself to struggle through the placid water. Just as daylight started to set in, she crawled out of the water and fainted, face down, in the sand. She shuddered as she recalled the ordeal. "Thank God for the fisherman," she murmured to herself. The policeman touched her on her shoulder and pointed to a landmass just to the right of the bow and told her arrangements had been made for them to continue to on to Tahiti by plane. "We should be there soon," he told her.

After the plane landed in the capital city of Pape'ete, Chrystal was taken to the US Consulate where, once again, she communicated what she had gone through for the past several weeks. She knew she had to endure the questioning and processing of the nightmare, but she was also tired of answering question after question that required her to relive the nightmare. She just wanted to see her family and go home. After what seemed like an eternity, the bureaucratic processing ended. She was advised that law enforcement and her family would be arriving tomorrow. She didn't look forward to another round of interviews with the police, but she also did not want Chris to escape punishment for what he did to her, or potentially to other unsuspecting victims. The one thing she wanted to do to end the day was take hot bath and sleep in a real bed.

The French authorities in coordination with the US Consulate had contacted a pilot of Air France flying out of Los Angeles and requested that once the plane landed, Chrystal's family should be the first to deplane. It was a like a magical moment when she saw the plane approach with her family aboard—who so many times she thought she'd never see again—about to land. The plane taxied to the customs area. The door opened and she saw her mom and dad, along with a policeman, starting to walk down the steps. As they approached the entrance to the terminal, they were greeted by Tahitian dancers and musicians welcoming them to the island. It was all so festive. The tears flowed and the hugging never seemed to stop. It was like they were afraid to let go of each other as the emotional reunion took place. The detective stood aside ready to go to work when it was timely.

CHAPTER 35

The rising sun, as it so often does, used the sky and clouds to create the start of the day with a sky with such beauty it compelled most people to take a few seconds to look at the artistic painting nature created for their enjoyment. The shafts of light reflecting off the white puffy clouds caused them, for a few brief minutes, to welcome the rays of the sun to create, to varying degrees, an enrichment of rose and pink transformation to take place. The colors were in a state of constant mutation that enhanced their beauty. It was a magnificent sight that artists could paint, but they are no match for the ultimate artist, Mother Nature. Chris, now on a westerly course, paid absolutely no attention to the artistry taking place in the tropical sky. He hoped he would find another island in the general area and soon. He was optimistic that other islands must be nearby. With the prow of the boat set in the direction he wanted, his mind reflected back to Chrystal getting safely off the boat and possibly making it to shore to find help. He was very upset with himself for not ending his affair with Chrystal as he should have. He erred and blundered by not feeding her to the sharks. That was all he could think about as he stood at the helm thinking about what he must do right now. As far as he was concerned, the sky above was not an artistic moment—it was gloomy and overcast.

On the third day of the depressing and lonely sail, he saw a disruption on the horizon that might have been the peak of a mountain. He adjusted the rudder, released more sail, and headed toward the irregularity he believed to be land. After a few hours of sailing, he was able to confirm that he was indeed approaching a fairly large island. He studied the sun, which was not quite over-head, and estimated that he had several hours of daylight before the sun slipped over the horizon. In preparation of going ashore, he started repairing the Zodiac that Chrystal had punctured. It was his plan to get on and off the island as fast as possible. His list of things to acquire was short. A compass, food, and water. The nearer he got to the island, he could see it was a fairly large town. He hoped there would be a maritime facility on the island. After locating the inlet to the lagoon, he motored to an unused buoy that was some distance from the shore and secured the boat. It was his intention to see as few people as possible and make his time on shore limited. Satisfied that the boat was safely tethered to the buoy, he lowered the Zodiac and shoved off to the shoreline.

Chris had anticipated that there might be a language problem, so he took a few pieces of the compass with him. He would show the parts to the clerk. It eliminated the effort to explain what he wanted if there was a language barrier. He quickly learned that there were no taxis or other means of public transportation, which caused him to spend more time on the island than he wanted. He also learned the name of the island: Raiatea. In under five hours, he was back at the Zodiac with all the items he needed. Once aboard the boat, he prepared to leave immediately. After passing through the pass way to the open sea, he headed north. It was a secure feeling to have a compass once again. The wind was brisk so he unfurled some sail and soon the island behind him faded away as he sailed off to nowhere.

As the bow slapped and sliced through the sea, it created a melodic and rhythmic beat that was constant and enjoyable. As Chris listened to the ocean's symphony, it relaxed him as he tried to come up with ideas on what was next on his personal agenda. Now alone—very much alone—he took solace in the fact that he would not be caught. A feeling of security, in his view, of any fear of being caught and punished was comforting. He remained in a reflective mood of relaxation and contemplation for some time. He had no idea how long he reflected on what to do next. Evening was starting to draw the curtain on the day, so he set the autopilot on a due north course and went below and went to bed alone, without Chrystal. Now below deck, he listened to the ocean's musical production. It was creating a mood of loneliness and solitude. The magic of music. It comforted him topside, but now it depressed him. Feelings of insecurity were starting to creep into his psyche and they were not welcomed. It was going to be a long night.

The morning of day four was like all the other countless days that followed. He was losing track of time. He started talking to himself. Asking questions and then answering them. His mind wouldn't give him any peace.

It caused him to continually ask questions, and more often than not, he did not like a lot of the answers. The same questions day after day and generally the same answers. He would be hard put to say what was the main and most troublesome concern, but the power of the Townsend family would be near the top of the list. If Chrystal managed to get to the island and get help, she would be home by now.

"Right, Chris?" he asked himself.

Reluctantly, he responded, "Probably." He generally talked out loud because he needed to hear the sound of a voice. So the questions flowed and the unwelcome answers continued.

The prolonged isolation and loneliness started eroding his mental health. He wasn't sure if it had been two weeks or three when he started sailing north. The days were long and the nights longer. Time was relative. He was no longer sure if his planning and abduction of Chrystal was as foolproof as he had thought. The one major mistake he made was letting her live. His insecurity increased expeditiously when he thought about what the Townsend family could do. There would be a large reward to find him and the boat. The amount would probably be over $100,000.

"Right, Chris?"

He agreed with himself. "I'm sure." With that kind of money available, the West Coast boating world would be on the lookout for him and his boat. Marinas from Mexico to the state of Washington would be on the alert. He raised his insecurity level even higher when he factored in the agencies that could or would be on the lookout for him.

As he was developing a checklist of things that might lead to his decision, the artistic skills of Chrystal came to mind. The police would not need to use an expert to draw a likeness of what he looks like. Chrystal had the skill to do it for them. She was always drawing and sketching subjects and did a good likeness of whatever the subject was. The more negative things he thought, the more serious and desperate his situation looked. He tried to comfort himself by saying, "Well, she really can't draw *that* well." Every time he thought of something that might cause him to be worried, he'd offset the thought with a what he thought would dispell it. Turn a negative into a positive. Standing at the helm with his arms on the wheel, he slumped over and stared at his feet. He didn't move or look up. He just stood there. He was tired. He was physically and emotionally spent. He knew and had to admit that he'd ruined his life, and his current situation had to come to a sad conclusion. He had no family, no friends, no home, nowhere to go, and probably his likeness would be on some of the TV networks, the internet, and posted on numerous bulletin boards. He didn't know what to do. He also knew he had to do something. Talking to his alter ego, he asked, "What?"

CHAPTER 36

From sunrise to sunset, the days seemed to take forever. Every day was like two days. Long and troublesome. He tried to keep track of how long it had been since the Ferrari Girl swam out of his life. He wasn't sure, and he wasn't sure if he really cared. He guessed two weeks, three weeks, maybe four. There was one thing that was a constant in his daily life, the directional reading on the compass. He kept the arrow pointing north. Today, the long "forty-eight-hour day," finally started to end as the sun's rays faded behind a light fog that blurred the horizon. He retired to the cabin for another night alone.

Sleep was difficult on this evening's sail because he and his alter ego had long and contentious conversations about what he should do to bring this phase of his life to some conclusion. The two debated back and forth throughout most of the night. He hardly got any sleep. He was exhausted when he went topside the next morning and was greeted by fog that encompassed the boat. It was fairly dense, but he estimated that it would burn off in a few hours. Despite getting very little sleep, he was energized on this dreary morning. The alter ego prevailed on what he must do.

Chris was correct about the fog dissipating. It thinned out quickly and visibility improved. He adjusted his direction so that he was on a northeastern tack. He wanted to see if his intuitive feeling or hunch was correct. After a few hours of sailing, he saw land. His hunch was right. To try and get his bearings, he carefully guided the boat toward the landmass ahead. The closer he got to what he saw, the more excited he became. It was the Coronado Islands just south of San Diego and off the coastline of Mexico. He had sailed to the islands many times with his family. He was pleased to know where he was, but it was a sad and touching time as well. The boat was now in the area where it had been found without anyone aboard. He was convinced that he was sailing over the graves of his mom and dad. It was a moving and chilling feeling. It was also time to follow through with what he had to do.

Now that he knew where he was, he adjusted the sails and the autopilot so that the boat was now sailing away from the islands. After being underway for a few hours, he lowered the sails and let the ocean move the boat as it wished. He was adrift. He had spent most of the day doing numerous adjustments to the boat. He had completed his tasks just before the day gave way to the thick fog that returned along with the darkness of night. He was ready. He walked to the rear of the boat and picked up the thick hemp rope that he and Chrystal used so many times to hold on to when they entered the water. He firmly gripped the rope and slipped into the water. He counted the seconds. When he got to fifty-five, he slowly released his grip on the rope and without fear allowed himself to be taken by the ocean to join the spirits of his beloved parents. He wanted atonement. Before he succumbed to unconsciousness, he spoke to his mom.

"Hold me. Love me. Forgive me." Those were his last words as his body and soul left the physical world and the sharks circled.

Five seconds after the ocean accepted Chris, one of the last flights allowed to take off due to the fog out of Los Angles was on a southern route when it passed over the Coronado Islands. The pilot thought he saw a blurred image that might be something on fire. He wasn't sure, but he relayed what he saw to the tower in San Diego. He gave them the longitude and latitude and continued his flight to Mexico. The information was passed along to the coast guard who said they would check the area after the fog lifted. A record of the location they had been given was checked some thirty-six hours later, and an entry in the file was recorded that they did not see anything that suggested a fire had taken place in the location provided.

Chris had spent his last day on the boat preparing for a massive fire to take place after he entered the ocean. He strategically placed lit candles throughout the boat near rags saturated with gasoline that would ignite once the flame and vapors met. He even adjusted the height of each candle so that they would start on fire at about the same time. He had arranged so many fire sites that the fire would be massive and destroy any trace of the boat. To try to attract sharks, he had collected fish he caught and chummed the water. He did not want his body found and plucked from the sea for identification. The only version of events would be Chrystal's, and she would not be able to provide facts that would support whatever she told the authorities. He ended his life believing that morally he could not be forgiven for what he had done, but the abduction of Chrystal would remain unprovable mystery.

The tête-à-tête with his alter ego convinced him that to try and elude the power of the Townsend family after they heard Chrystal's account of what happened would be a living hell. He would probably be caught and receive a severe punishment that would cause him to live most if not all his life in a prison cell.

"Do not let that happen. Do what you have to do to," his other self said, and he did.

CHAPTER 37

Before Chrystal had left French Polynesia, the *Malibu Times* headlines read TOWNSEND GIRL FOUND SAFE AND ALIVE. The article went on to say that the sheriff's department was very guarded in what they would release to the press while they conducted their investigation.

During their contacts with Chrystal, the detectives ran into dead end after dead end trying to establish who was responsible for what happened to her. After a few weeks had passed, they asked for the public's help. Composite drawings and the name of Chis (if that was his real name) appeared often in the paper, but no viable leads developed. As time went by without any significant progress, the case lost its frontpage coverage and eventually was seldom mentioned. The sheriff had his best staff on the case, but to his dismay, the matter was heading in the direction of becoming a cold case. It was mystifying, challenging, and frustrating to the investigators. Chrystal, on the other hand, was not upset with their lack of progress in trying to find and arrest Chris. She actually felt sorry for him. He tried to ruin her life, but in actuality, she survived a stronger person. She knew he was a weak and insecure person and that he would not be able to hold up under the strain of being a hunted and wanted kidnapper as well as a rapist. Somewhere, somehow, something will end Chris's ability to exist. He may have thought he committed the perfect crime and would never be caught, but did he?

Time in its inexorable way helped heal some of the past for Chrystal. She decided to delay advanced study abroad at Oxford and became involved in helping out other women who had trouble coping with traumatic life experiences. Her experience was so powerful and compelling that it served her well in helping other women. It was satisfying and it also helped her as she helped others.

One morning as she and her mom were sitting on the veranda having their morning coffee, the landline phone rang. Chrystal answered it.

"Hello?"

"Is this Chrystal?"

"Yes, who's this?"

"It's Joachim. I'm calling from France. Remember me?"

"Yes, of course."

He had recently learned of her experience and read about her swim to safety. From that point on, the conversation was more about catching up what they had been doing since their time as students in college. She learned that he was the owner of two wineries in the Bordeaux area. She also learned that he still liked to swim, but only recreationally. Before they terminated the phone call, he asked her if she would like to be his guest in the immediate future and visit him and his parents. They both got a laugh when he suggested, "Let's go for a swim." The long call ended with her accepting the invitation with the caveat, "No sailboat trips. I'll bring a bathing suit." A future date was set for the visit. Chrystal was excited.

CHAPTER 38

The editor of the *Malibu Times* looked up when a recently hired cub reporter entered his office and asked him if he had time to discuss a story he was thinking about writing.

"Of course, what about?" he asked.

"The Townsend girl's alleged story about her being kidnapped and mistreated."

"You think there is a story there?"

"Well, everything we know about the case is what she said. No proof has been established that substantiates her account of events. Maybe she got involved in a situation that went bad and she concocted a story where the blame for her absence was placed on a bad guy named Chris. What you think?"

"Mmmm. I don't know. Let me think about it and I'll get back to you."

"Thanks. Oh, by the way, I called her yesterday and left a message. I called back this morning and learned she left for France last night."

"Interesting."

THE END